# MAJI

### THE UNTOLD ADVENTURE OF THE MEN OF THE EAST

L M MEIER

iUniverse, Inc.
Bloomington

# MAJI
**The untold adventure of the men of the East**

*iUniverse books may be ordered through booksellers or by contacting:*

*iUniverse*
*1663 Liberty Drive*
*Bloomington, IN 47403*
*www.iuniverse.com*
*1-800-Authors (1-800-288-4677)*

*ISBN: 978-1-4620-5916-4 (sc)*
*ISBN: 978-1-4620-5917-1 (ebk)*

*Library of Congress Control Number: 2011918130*

*Printed in the United States of America*

*iUniverse rev. date: 10/20/2011*

*For Daniel*

*"We were not wise. We were not kings.
We were men."*

*Zebedeo of Tayma, circa 4 B.C.*

# PROLOGUE

*When I was a young man, my father taught me that everyone has the capacity for good or evil and a single act can create life or destroy it. What distinguishes us from those who seek evil rests in our ability to act righteously in the face of death. This simple lesson altered my life in one of the darkest moments I've ever witnessed. My name is Zebedeo. I am the son of the Ma-ji.*

# MARKETPLACE

## TAYMA VILLAGE, ABOUT 4 B.C.

My father is an accomplished mathematician and star-gazer. In his mind, it didn't matter how well I studied or mastered my lessons, there was always room for improvement. Perhaps I never measured up to the great men of his family. In his defense, he sacrificed a lot for those he loved. And while part of him resented living in a small village instead of the grand city of Jerusalem, the other part loved Tayma because it was the birthplace of my mother and he loved her dearly. When I was about ten, she died from a terrible fever. Since that time my father lost his desire to travel extensively as he had so fervently done in the past. And while most of my life has been spent in this little desert village, I have benefited. I learned the teachings of wise men from the great northern cities, those from the south toward the great pyramids, and later from the men of the orient. Despite the scale and intrigue of the cities, Tayma is the place I prefer most, feeling content with its small group of humble villagers and living in its peaceful landscape. We also enjoy many freedoms that the people of the great city do not. There are fewer rules to confine us and quite frankly, in a town where a variety of travelers stop in to rest briefly and then move on, we are well situated to accept almost anyone.

Our land rests in the north-west Arabian Peninsula in the Province of Tabuk where the climate is warm and hospitable and surrounded by the majestic *Jabal Ghunaym* Mountains. As a boy I found many distractions and met interesting people passing through our sweet oasis and the well at *Bir Hadaj*. Legend has it that water from the *Bir Hadaj* provides to its drinkers illuminations, prophesies and great wisdom. It stands tall in the city center bordered by a lush palm garden. This place is home to tradesmen, artisans, a few farmers, and the local priests. It is a place of enchantment and a place for dreamers like me.

Men here like my father Majid, follow the Zoroastrian faith steeped in the science of the stars which has been handed down through many generations. Since as far back as I can remember, we have spoken many languages and studied many philosophies. As a child I learned from the men in my village who spoke the words of the travelers—men who came to Tayma to rest and drink of the *Bir Hadaj*. In a single day I might meet men from five different tribes—a Helene, a Roman, a Chaldean, an Egyptian, or a Hebrew. Many have noble ideas on business and commerce, some are slaves, some are soldiers, and others are mere messengers passing through.

The day that Majid and I returned home together from the marketplace was one that I remember vividly. I was only beginning to understand myself in the way that a young man discovers his place in a larger world. And this was the year that I discovered much about my destiny. It was the year that my father began traveling again and it gave us great joy to embark on the first of many as father and son. We had just purchased supplies for the journey across the great desert, and like many fathers before him, Majid wanted the best for me but often had trouble expressing it.

"Zebedeo, it has come to my attention that you have not minded your studies and have too much interest in these—*tecknos* that seem to occupy so much of your time."

"We've already had this conversation father."

"You must be able to work without these devices as someday they will fail you." Majid added. "And then what will you do?"

"A thousand times father, enough!"

But Majid was relentless and not easily dissuaded when he had a lesson to give his only son. I had studied countless hours, more so than any boy my age. In fact, while my peers were maneuvering hills and fashioning swords or recreating some historical battle, I was often inside reading another compendium my father had collected for me. It was aggravating. I wanted to know the stars, but I struggled with my desire to be more.

"Zebedeo, I feel you are lazy and stubborn and it disrespects me."

"These objects are the future father. The men of the new world will be great because of them. Does not a farmer benefit from a superior axe or plow? It is not from laziness that makes his workday shorter; but improved tools that make his life better."

This remark put him over the edge and only escalated his anger.

"I am sick of this discussion Zebedeo," his tone growing louder. He paced back and forth, tugging his beard, frowning down at the ground. "A boy must follow in his father's place. There is no compromise. And the old ways must not be forgotten!"

"Father, I have studied the old ways. As a child I put them to my mind. But a man must move away from boyish things." Immediately I realized that my words did not come out the way I had intended.

"Boyish?!" he said appearing shocked.

The affect of my words were visible by his wounded expression. But I knew my father well enough to know that his dramatic reactions were often used to gain the upper hand in an argument and as a distraction against an adversary.

"Go! Go to the house and prepare for our journey," he shouted. "Leave me or we shall just make each other angry!"

I started for home. After a moment I glanced back and saw that he had moved to sit on a nearby bench. Concerned, I quickly returned to his side.

"Are you alright father?"

"Go ahead Zebedeo," he replied calmly and waving me onward. "I will follow soon."

His tone had quickly changed and he no longer appeared angry with me. Instead, he merely sat, deep in thought. Without more than a moment's pause, he rose, fully capable.

As he adjusted his robe two men approached, each man accompanied by an attendant and pack animal. I recognized their rich dress and saw that they were a Babylonian priest and a Chinese nobleman. The Babylonian was strong and young—with fierce eyes and large muscles. He had a beauty in his countenance—noble, clean, and elegant. He wore a royal blue silk sash trimming his chest and edged in the brightest gold and his garments where the whitest and cleanest I had ever seen, like clouds. His shirt opened to vent himself from the hot sun and his skin showed the richness of his color. He was fearsome and majestic, like an ancient god.

The Chinese nobleman was firm and lean and not unpleasant to look upon. His eyes were dark and slender, his appearance healthy and upright. His dress was ornate and regal and the patterns of his garments where the brightest red, yellow, and wine. He wore a delicate sash cord that appeared like spun gold tied around his waist. Upon his head was a headdress in a style that I had not seen before, tightly fitted with golden ornaments. The man's garments however, appeared too heavy for our climate and seemed to cause him some fatigue.

"Is that you Majid?" The god-like priest roared. "I thought I smelled the foul scent of an old dog."

Instead of properly addressing my father, the man pushed Majid as he passed, setting him off balance. I could sense the tension rising.

"Balthazar, you skinny desert rat!"

Majid tried to push Balthazar in return but the man hardly moved. Soon, and without any further words, the men made their way through the marketplace cautiously watching the other while their eyes quickly scanned every merchant cart and shopkeeper. I stared in curiosity at what one might have in store for the other. Then Balthazar rolled a basket into Majid's path and Majid countered by toppling a collection of fruit under Balthazar's feet. Liu Shang, Balthazar's companion, perhaps feeling left out of the competition, escalated the game by ejecting a section of fabric in the air that swirled in the way a water snake glides upon the lake. In a momentary pause above, the fabric unfolded then fell upon Balthazar's head.

"What is this mischief?" Balthazar exclaimed. "Two against one? Give up Liu Shang or I will shame you before your servants."

"You may be strong Balthazar," said Liu Shang" "but I am as quick as a vapor. I will disappear before your eyes."

Liu Shang pulled a small shiny object from his sleeve and tossed it into the air. Just as Balthazar had removed the cloth from his face, the tiny object popped into a small brilliant flash that temporarily impaired Balthazar's vision. I had heard of exploding powders of the east but had never seen anything like this. I wondered whether to turn around and go back to them but the view from the wall at the edge of the marketplace was too good a perch to give up so easily. I climbed up the stone stairway and stood on the riser to watch.

"Let's see you vanish," Balthazar said. "And I won't need your magic to make you disappear," he chuckled.

Balthazar threw the fabric down and started after Liu Shang who was well ahead. The warrior-priest approached the produce merchant and selected the fattest, juiciest piece of fruit, and quickly hurled it into the air across a great distance. It ricocheted between the merchant stands heading in some unknown direction. I saw Liu Shang crouching as if by his expression he was sure to be protected behind one of the merchant carts. Just as he started to rise and sure that the threat had passed, the piece of fruit burst upon his clothes and Balthazar laughed heartily. As Balthazar brushed his hands together in satisfaction, proud of his retaliatory strike, Majid was contemplating some sort of retribution. The old man wandered a bit further and tapped his walking stick on a cage of doves, releasing them. Suddenly, the birds flew wildly toward Balthazar and nearly toppled him over.

"A warrior-priest defeated by a few doves?" teased Liu Shang as he wandered ahead of Balthazar.

I jumped down from the stone riser and walked a few paces toward home. I couldn't help but shake my head at the site of them. But this was their way. The depth of their friendship was demonstrated through practical jokes and playful competition. By this time Majid had joined me at the gates to our land and we watched as the two foreign noblemen approached.

Balthazar quickly moved his supplies to one arm and with the other drew his scimitar. He crept up behind Liu Shang who was a few steps ahead and with a swordsman's skill slid the scimitar under the silk cord holding up the Chinaman's pants. One quick tug was all that was needed. The pants immediately fell to the ground and Liu Shang was left standing—holding on to his supplies in embarrassment causing everyone, including the attendants to laugh.

After a moment, Balthazar, Liu Shang and the small caravan of men and pack animals, met us on the path and we walked up to the garden entrance. Our house was a fine stone building with details and ornamentation—regal enough for my father yet simple and refined like my mother. It was a spacious residence with gardens, a pasture and small farm extending beyond the walls. I had a few words with our guest's attendants and they led the animals toward the stables. I turned to see my father and Balthazar embrace. They had shared many adventures together in their youth with Majid mentoring Balthazar like a son. Now, Balthazar was a great spiritual man in his own right. He gained the respect of many wherever he traveled—perhaps his good looks and physical strength were a factor. I admired him.

"Majid, Zebedeo," Balthazar greeted, "may I present my friend from the east, Master Liu Shang."

"Despite Balthazar's unorthodox ways," replied Majid, "we accept his friends as our own. Welcome to Tayma."

Liu Shang bowed and to the easterner's surprise, my father gave him a familiar embrace.

As the wise men entered the house I could not help but smile for in that instant, it felt as if our family was reunited.

# TABLE OF ELDERS
## Tayma Country House

After ensuring the attendants were settled in the servants quarters and instructing our chief attendant Ra-bi of his tasks during our journey, I started back toward the house to join the men who were likely having some wine and telling a few overblown tales from their past. But as I entered, I heard something I had not expected.

"Majid, you can no longer think of him as a boy," said Balthazar as I stopped in the entryway. "He has a tremendous gift and he must be allowed to lead us."

"He is not ready," Majid insisted. "He spends his time dawdling with odd pieces of wood and metal. I cannot deter him."

As I entered, the room fell into an awkward silence. Our servants brought in meats, fragrant sauces, and candied fruit trays to the table. I joined the men and reclined on a low sofa padded with an enormity of my father's favorite pillows and stacks of family manuscripts that towered around us.

It was easy to discern that there were no women in residence. Our home had none of the refining touches that a woman could add—the perfumed oils, the silken ornaments, nor the sweetly arranged flowers. We did however, have the pleasure of a delicious jasmine tea that I sipped most curiously. It was a gift from Liu Shang who also brought several medicinal elixirs from the East and several powders that produced the explosion I had observed in the marketplace.

After we dined and our places cleared, our visitors recounted their travels and explained how the heavens had guided them to a village in *Xingjian* where they had met. Liu Shang had been star-watching intently for months until he met Balthazar. The men quickly became friends and decided to seek the great Majid to inquire about a very extraordinary star that both men had observed.

Balthazar and my father laid-out a large celestial map on the table. The hand painted detail was unmatched—created by my father when he was a young man. He always took pride in his craftsmanship and pointed out every fine detail in the relief and the amount of time and perfection a work of this magnitude required. I couldn't help but smile as I watched him tell his map making tale for the one-hundredth time.

"It is a fine work," remarked Balthazar.

"It *is* a fine piece, though I do say so myself." Majid replied.

The firelight from the corner of the room illuminated the space and cast a warm glow over both conversation and countenance as we studied in preparation for the coming journey.

"Liu Shang, tell us of your country," I asked. "I have heard that there are many Chinese mysteries concerning the heavens."

"Your question shows much wisdom Zebedeo," Liu Shang replied. "A great mathematician in my country said that several new stars appeared for a time then vanished. And I myself have seen others, not previously witnessed by the ancients. This is a great mystery."

"The Chinese are very wise in their study," said Balthazar. "We Zoroastrians have a few heavenly mysteries as well."

"Indeed," replied Majid sensing his cue. "Come my friends."

As the men rose, I took two of my instruments and followed along. We walked down a narrow corridor of our house. This was a corridor I had not ventured down in a very long time. My father picked up the small lamp from the stone ledge and as he led the way, he lighted another lamp and placed it back on another small stone ledge. As we followed, he lit the second, third, and continued until all twelve lamps were lit casting a beautiful glow down the corridor. The lamps sat six on each side with each lamp signifying a different constellation. At the end of the stone hallway was a large wooden door. I took the small lamp from my father's hand as he attempted to pull the door open. But it did not yield.

"A bit rusty," he replied, smiling at Balthazar.

"Yes you are old man," said Balthazar smiling back at his host.

The warrior-priest then stepped forward and with very little effort, he pulled the heavy doors open. I returned the small lamp to my father and we entered the cool and dark room.

With the lamp in hand, Majid lit a small wick perched near the entrance. The fire took up the wick and traveled onward and upward, revealing a long slender oil canal that spiraled up and around the vast domed room. As the light flowed, the room, once dark, now displayed the volume, scale and ornamentation of the mosaics around us. Inlaid in the floor was a map of the region, detailed with colored tiles, shiny stones, and bits of colored glass to identify landmarks, villages, and cities. Above us, the great dome was painted an azure blue, like the great expanse of sky, and inlaid in the ceiling were clear glass stones to mark the constellations that flickered in the delicately burning lights.

"Some stars, like this one in the Whale, are brighter than ever," said Majid pointing upward, "while others, like this one in the Great Bear, are losing their brilliance."

"And a great many change without warning." Balthazar added. After a moment, Balthazar turned to me.

"Zebedeo, tell us what you know of the great star."

"I have calculated the triangulation of the great star with this instrument," I replied pulling the small device from my belt and demonstrating to the elders. "I call it a star-guide."

Majid just coughed and looked away. He was skeptical of the entire idea of using tools to measure what man should plainly observe with his own eyes.

"I met a Hellene with an object like that," replied Balthazar. "An *astroloke*, I believe he said."

"Has this instrument changed your opinion of the sky?" asked Liu Shang.

"Yes," I replied. "The star has remained stationary from night to night, never changing its parallax, so it must lie far away."

"Balthazar has told me of your artistry." said Liu Shang. "And what is this?" said Liu Shang looking at the small brass scope I held.

"I've been working on a device that may increase the visibility of the stars," I instructed. "This simple cylinder helps but I cannot locate a glass stone clear enough to improve the view."

Majid was visibly irritated and walked away as if interested in something at the other side of the room.

"These are fine for your idle time my son. But a man of the stars cannot rely upon them. Our methods have been handed down through the ages—generation to generation; priest to priest. And we all know that a truly wise man needs only the heavens to guide him."

"You are right, of course father." I admitted.

"But there are many wise men who seek it," Balthazar proclaimed, "and yet they have not a fraction of the knowledge of this young man."

"This is a star that became so brilliant that it surpassed the brightness of Venus or Mercury," I continued, "and is visible on the meridian even by day."

Liu Shang, who had stooped to examine the floor map, rose with excitement. "It is the King Star!" he blurted.

The men gathered beside me. They smiled and nodded to each other, highly intrigued. My father was caught up in the excitement too and joined us immediately.

"How many men search for its meaning?" I asked intently of my father.

I was eager to start our journey and wanted to make certain my elders knew that I took this task seriously.

"I am unsure," replied Majid. "There could be many."

"In the East there is much talk of the birth of the Deliverer," Balthazar added.

"A King of all kings they say," said Liu Shang becoming anxious. "We must take precautions. An event like this could attract murderers and profit seekers."

"Fear profits a man nothing," Balthazar soothed. "But faith brings a man to boldness."

"You will lead us then Majid?" Liu Shang implored.

"Indeed," said Majid having pondered the question for a moment. "Let us make ready."

Balthazar smiled a faint smile at me and slapped his hand on my shoulder. It was as if the weight of a large tree had been laid upon me for I had not been prepared for his grasp. My startled expression must have amused him for he bellowed his hearty laugh and walked with me out of the room. It was good to see that the men were pleased with the plan. We parted company to mind our own duties and retire for the evening before beginning the journey.

I left the house to speak to Ra-bi one last time. All seemed ready and our supplies and equipment were adequate. As for our spirits, that was another matter. There was a decidedly new energy in all of us. It had been an eventful day and while I returned to my room, I knew sleeping would be difficult. The evening was warm and a gentle breeze blew through the window to my chamber. The winds seemed to reflect my restlessness. I walked to the balcony and climbed up the ladder, perching myself upon the roof. Up there, I was left to my thoughts and dreams. I had spent countless hours in quiet meditation there. Before the expanse above I knelt in prayer.

"God in heaven if in your mercy you can hear me, please be with us on our journey."

I was neither a philosopher nor an ideal man of prayer, but I did believe in something. What that something was, I did not fully understand.

"Please find us worthy of your blessing. Please send to us your new king and bring peace to all nations."

Observing the major stars before me and seeing the great star in the distance only caused me more anxiety about what was to come. I was a believer in many things.

For one, I knew that if a man had decided upon a task, he could accomplish it—whatever the purpose. Balthazar and I discussed this many times. He called it 'free will.' And while I understood most of his teachings, there were things that I simply could not reconcile—like the idea of a singular, powerful, and unseen creator. I liked things I could see—the stars, the fields, the mountains, people, and the instruments I invented. The possibilities were boundless in the things men could create and I had hoped to create the tools to improve not only our study of the heavens, but improve our lives as well. A noble mission, I thought.

That night I lay restless in my bed, wanting to depart sooner than we had originally planned. But we had agreed to four hours rest. Not that it helped me. I was too excited. We would explore new lands and visit places that I had not traveled in years. Time in the company of men in the wilderness meant learning their ways—something I had long wanted to do. I also imagined that the familiar places in Jerusalem would be just as enjoyable as before. I had spent a short time there years ago with my young cousins and we explored the marketplace, played in the wheat fields outside the city, and climbed to the roof tops to look upon the vast sea of buildings. We were kings on the mountain top and didn't get into too much trouble—though my cousin Omar and I met-up with some minor trouble once. One spring I broke a potter's vase while trying to sling a rock at a turtledove. Other than the four coppers it cost my father, it was harmless. Naturally, my father didn't forget the incident very quickly and was faithful to remind me of how irresponsible it was to sling rocks within the city walls. He was right of course.

As my thoughts returned to our trip, I wondered what sort of people I would encounter. Would I meet the new king that the star had announced? Would the Roman presence in Jerusalem delay our travel? I had developed a keen interest in examining Roman inventions since my last visit. What sort of new machines had they created? I could not help but imagine.

Many of my father's previous trips through the desert would start at night and this was no exception. It would however, be a fine opportunity to test my new tools and refine my skills with the star-gazer. While I did thirst for a bit of adventure, it was likely to be an uneventful one. And once we returned, things would remain the same as always. My father would complain and I would probably give up my interest in developing small machines. On the other hand, traveling gave us the opportunity to see the inventions others have developed and giving me more ideas could lead to some trouble at home. But even if there was any real trouble, there was nothing to worry about. Balthazar was with us.

# ROAD TO THE HOLY CITY

## SOUTHEAST OF TAYMA

We made our way toward Jerusalem and it was a favorably cool night. Everyone in our party rode a camel except Balthazar. His mount was an Arabian steed he named Eclipse, a lovely ornamented beast elegant enough for short rides but a questionable choice for such a long journey through the desert. As his name suggested, Eclipse was a black stallion with a fine linear circle of white on one of his hindquarters resembling the same lunar event. Steps behind the *Ma-ji*, I led our small caravan comprised of eight attendants and a dozen or so pack camels. It was a great journey to pay homage to the new king, I thought, and marked by the great star before us. I had never met a king in all of my life and the excitement coursed through my blood.

The roads were relatively desolate this time of year though on occasion the scenery was punctuated with a few foreigners visible in the distance. But the time passed quickly and after several days travel, we were not far from Jerusalem. Each afternoon we would camp and by night the men would tell stories. I frequently roamed from one group to another. First, I'd check in with Ra-bi to make certain he had prepared things for the following day's journey. Then generally, I would join my father and the *Ma-ji* to listen to their discussions of some adventure they had encountered in their youth or hear the story of some lovely woman they had seen in a distant land. Many nights played out in the simple rituals we shared—attending to the animals, bathing to wash off the sand, spending a few quiet moments in prayer, and preparing a light meal around the evening fire. In the company of these great men I often felt like an infant. My heart however, was stirring in a way that I had not yet understood. I was nearly a man, but in mind and manner I was boyish in so many ways. I felt that I'd never live up to my father's expectations as a scholar. But the truth be known, I really didn't want to follow exactly in his footsteps. I wanted to do things my own way. Even so, the night sky beckoned me to join the league of the brave and noble *Ma-ji* and I could feel its force tugging at my soul in the way the moon pulls the tide.

In the darkness of the early morning, we resumed our travel before the sun rose to its height. As it grew hotter, most of us were lost in our own delirious thoughts about the Holy City and its history. And as the sun rose that day, we felt a liveliness that rallied our spirits. Balthazar, a man I had known since my childhood, was like an older brother to me. He often rode at the front of the caravan with the elders. While I was permitted to ride alongside them, I was unsure about whether I should. It seemed to be Balthazar's accepted place. I rode just behind them and managed the rest of the caravan without much notice from my father. As we rode on, Balthazar fell back from the front of the company and approached me.

"I thought to speak plainly to you Zebedeo. And this is as good a time as any," he said. "What is this rift I sense in your father's affection?"

I signed and attempted to explain as honestly as possible but without dishonoring my father.

"My father is like an old woman," I joked. "He complains about everything I do."

"It is a father's job to train his son in the way that he should go. Your father is a wise man Zebedeo. You should take his lessons with gladness for he will not be with you forever."

"I'm not sure if he fears these things for me or for himself," I said with half a thought.

"Perhaps it is a little of both. He does not understand what you do with instruments and tools," said Balthazar. "For a wise man with many credits to his name, this is difficult."

"What was your father like?" I asked.

"When I was about your age, I told my parents that I wanted to serve in the army. My noble family would not allow me to be a common soldier and reprimanded me for considering the work of a slave. They believed it would shame them."

"That's why you are a priest?"

"I am a priest because I am a Zurvan of Babylon," said Balthazar.

"It is your lot," I said making more of a statement than asking a question.

Balthazar smiled.

"Not exactly Zebedeo." He began. "I chose this life of my own free will. A great tenet of the Zoroastrian faith is the idea that we are not at the mercy of the fates, but we choose for ourselves.

I stared at him blankly.

"But enough of that for now," he offered. "Let me go and see what trouble I can cause your father." Not waiting for my reply, Balthazar rode to rejoin the elders.

I realized that we were not far from Jerusalem just as a flock of small songbirds flew overhead. A marked change in the landscape lay before us with a few shade trees and bushes along the roadway. Small animals darted across our path and caused the camels to flinch, hiss, and behave nervously. Liu Shang's camel became agitated and broke off a piece of the *Fasoot,* a sweet smelling berry bush known in the region for its dark shiny leaves and small orange-colored fruit.

"I caution you my friend, you may wish to keep your camel away from that plant," said Majid. "The consequences could be undesirable."

I'm not sure whether Liu Shang understood my father as he raised a quizzical brow. But the man from the east merely nodded then returned to his daydreams. This was the familiar time in a trip across the desert that everyone in the company was sluggish. The men were lost in thought, partially because they wanted to conserve water and were not drinking enough, and partially, because the air was warmer and drier this time of day. It was the time of day that literally drained you of energy.

As the sun peered over the hills, we approached a narrow passageway against jagged, rocky peaks. Balthazar joined Majid at the front of the caravan. Knowing that Majid loved to lead, Balthazar teasingly tried to take it from him. As the sun began to rise over the rocky hills before us, the light gently peered through the pass casting a heavenly glow to our path.

"Behold my friends," Majid announced. "The Eye of the Needle."

"Breathtaking!" replied Liu Shang.

"Do you know why it is said that a rich man cannot pass through the Eye of the Needle?" asked Majid.

"I do not know this saying" Liu Shang replied.

"It is because thieves and murders will kill anyone who passes this way—especially a rich man," Majid laughed.

We passed a decaying horse along the roadside. The flies had overtaken the carcass and Liu Shang became uneasy.

"The land may kill us first," he said.

"Perhaps he was a rich horse," I replied hoping to lighten the tension.

At the front of the pack Majid became increasingly annoyed with Balthazar who had moved to the head of the caravan.

"Zebedeo! Keep the watch," said Majid in frustration. "The hills are swarming with bloodthirsty thieves like Kahim Rajim."

I placed my hand on my scimitar. "Let them come. I am ready."

The area was known for its share of villainy. Merchants entering Jerusalem to trade were often accosted by at least a few outcasts now and then. But rarely was anyone murdered—so long as you had something of value to give away. It wasn't until now that I realized that my sword was much smaller than the other men's—certainly small compared to Balthazar's. My father's joke was timely because little did we know, a band of derelicts led by the infamous Kahim Rajim rested upon a nearby ridge and were interested in our small company.

"They're almost to the city," announced Kahim, high on a nearby hill. "Wake up you lazy swine. We must attack now!"

The thieves, many of whom had been sleeping, reluctantly assembled. They staggered to mount a mix of mangy camels and old horses and started down the rocky pass toward our caravan.

Meanwhile, Majid was occupied by the fact that Balthazar was taunting him and took the lead of the caravan. In brute force, he was no match for Balthazar, but in using his wisdom, he often won.

"Camels are the only beasts fit for the desert my friend," said Majid to distract him. "So why do you ask your horse to do a camel's job?"

"Eclipse is a warrior among horses."

As Balthazar spoke, Majid turned to see the thieves in the distance.

"Yes, but is he a warrior among thieves?!" replied Majid.

Majid had looked astonished. Balthazar, puzzled at his friend's expression, looked in the same direction. Noticing the men turn their eyes to the hills, the rest of us followed and watched as the band of thieves raced toward us.

"Kahim Rajim!" I yelled.

"Get the men through the pass!" cried Majid taking control of the situation.

Visibly unaccustomed to such an encounter, Liu Shang whipped his camel and fled toward the pass—alone.

"Quickly! Come quickly my friends," cried Liu Shang nearly falling from the camel.

"You must slow down Liu Shang." said Majid but the wise man from the East could not hear and was headed directly for the narrow passage riding his heavily packed beast.

"Ra-bi," I ordered. "Gather the other attendants and ride toward the Eye of the Needle." Ra-bi was quick to act.

He organized the others and set off after Majid and Liu Shang. Balthazar and I circled behind to meet the thieves. I drew my scimitar.

"Put away your sword Zebedeo," instructed Balthazar. "We are priests not mercenaries."

"Are we to pray our way out of this?" I replied.

"You are an inventor of tools. Invent!"

Balthazar pulled a staff from the last camel in the caravan and rode toward the mob of thieves. I followed. In man-to-man encounters, Balthazar quickly knocked two men from their mounts with the length of his staff. I was struggling with one thief whom I could not knock from his mangy horse. Balthazar knocked him down too and turned to me.

"You should ride a horse Zebedeo."

"Why?" I asked.

"A man is guided by the laws of God but . . ."

He was starting one of his long-winded sermons again—not that I didn't like to hear him speak, he was a great speaker and teacher, but now was not the time. I pointed behind him and motioned for him to look. The next group of thieves where about to strike.

"Balthazar," I interjected. But he would not be interrupted.

" . . . only through his free will does he choose to follow," he continued. "He must decide! And in similar fashion, a horse allows a certain freedom of . . ."

Before Balthazar could finish his sentence, I shouted, "Your back!"

Without turning, he extended his staff with a twirl striking his aggressors—hurling the men from their camels but killing no one.

As this was happening Kahim raced past us heading toward the pass and the caravan. Most of the men in our company had reached the Eye and dismounted. They threw garments over their camel's eyes and led the animals through safely. Liu Shang was a brave but slightly impatient man, and in his haste to rush everyone through, had managed to get his animal's packing caught between some jagged rocks that protruded from the walls. We rode quickly to catch up.

"You neglected to mention that a rich man cannot pass through the Eye of the Needle unless he dismounts his camel or unloads some of his pack!" scolded Liu Shang.

"Try harder to move your animal forward," Majid said shortly.

My father dismounted and took charge of the situation despite the growing fear in the attendants.

"You there in front, cover the beast's eyes and pull him through now!"

The attendant tried to pull the camel but the animal wouldn't move forward and Kahim was nearly upon them. Balthazar and I were riding to help, whipping our beasts onward, their hooves pounding and chests heaving. It was as if Liu Shang and my father were completely oblivious to the fact that Kahim was closing in. They remained occupied with unbridling the situation before them. With their backs turned to the impending danger, their scientific minds prevailed and their focus concerned the unsolved mystery of how a certain camel's pack might be dislodged. Liu Shang still mounted, called out to Majid but his words were inaudible in the chaos. Finally, Majid must have sensed that something was wrong. As Kahim raised his sword to strike from the rear, Majid immediately moved to the side of the animal and covered himself. Balthazar and I feared the worst. Just then, the beast made a loud groan and out of his behind shot a long wet spray of foulness that consumed Kahim and his nag from head to toe—stopping them in their tracks.

"Liu Shang can thank his beast for eating the desert berries," said Balthazar.

The camel now relieved, seemed to slip through the passageway. Kahim soon fled in disgust while the men in the caravan cheered and shook their fists at him. Majid turned around to see what had happened, almost unaware of Kahim's threat. He shrugged his shoulders, mounted his camel, and began to lead the caravan away. Balthazar and I chased after a few remaining thieves but after a while, we gave up the pursuit and turned back toward Jerusalem.

# JERUSALEM
## CITY OF WONDER

The men drove the caravan into the city quickly, still excited by the near-death experience. Balthazar and I had joined them and gradually slowed through the winding streets ourselves. Most of the servants, who had not seen such a great city before, were captivated by its vibrancy. The Jerusalem marketplace was far greater than anything in Tayma and was perceived as the center for everything imaginable. Lavish merchandise was bought and sold—the exotic and the rare, the ordinary and plain were set up by the shopkeepers. There were stands with fresh foods and flowers, exotic animals and wild birds, other shops displayed fine linens, and a blacksmith flanked a sword maker, and a jeweler was coupled with a goldsmith. Marked by the complexities of social and political expectations and limited by their standing in the order of things, people of different cultures, tongues, and customs came from distant places in the hopes of trade, prosperity, and worship.

As we rode through the residential districts, I observed the communities segregated by tribe and countrymen;

Romans in one section, Hellenes that the Romans called Greeks in another, Arabians in one quarter, Hebrews in yet another. The lines were more distinct than I had recalled in my youth and the city's population had multiplied. As we traveled through the narrow streets for some time, we passed a doorway bearing a huddled group of children. The eldest boy was about 13 years old. His delicate face stared at the *Ma-ji*. An even younger boy stood with his sister at the roadside. The tiny girl, looking half starved, held out her little hand to beg. The *Ma-ji* passed without notice—after all there was much to distract. I noticed; I could not help it. I tossed the children my small pack of food.

"What is your name boy?" I asked.

"I am Jacob. My brother there is Joshua," the young boy said pointing to his older brother. The boy Joshua bowed in gratitude.

As I turned to ride on, I held the glimpse of a beautiful girl with hair the color of the great cedars of Lebanon. But clearly she was not Phoenician—not in this section of the city. She came to the doorway and directed the children inside. Our eyes met but I had to look away and ride on. It was expected. It would be improper to look at her. Yet for some reason I didn't care about the custom. My modern upbringing in Tayma was to blame. I looked back anyway. She had paused and smiled before closing the door. It was a smile that could easily stop the hearts of men.

Rejoining our group, I traveled a few paces forward to the center of the city where we stopped at a large and beautiful home, ornate with pillars, golden details, fountains, and flowers. Immediately upon our arrival, several elegantly dressed servants met us at the footsteps and helped us dismount and took charge of the rest of the caravan.

"What is this place?" asked Liu Shang.

"The house of my brother Gaspar who is the King's High Treasurer," Majid replied. "We will take rest here."

Omar, my cousin approached the group as the men dismounted and smoothed their robes.

"Greetings cousin!" I said.

"Zebedeo!" cried Omar.

"You're just as I remember Omar. I see your mother's cooking is as fine as ever."

"My size is truly my uncle's fault. I think he told my mother she has a growing boy and she's never put the idea out of her mind."

"How is your mother?" I asked.

While I was reunited with my young cousin, Gaspar, flanked by two servants, exited the house and walked down the marble steps. He greeted Majid. Unlike my father's more muscular build, Gaspar was very slim and noble in appearance—meek and cautious when it came to speaking in groups of people, but a very loyal and reliable man.

"Brother, Majid, and let me see, Zebedeo," said Gaspar embracing me, "my, my, no longer a boy. And what a fine man you've become."

"Hello Gaspar," I replied.

"Majid, your family has exceeded all of our expectations," said Gaspar. "You must be very proud."

"Thank you brother," replied Majid. "Please join me in welcoming our friends—Balthazar, a Zoroastrian of great fame."

"Greetings Gaspar," replied Balthazar as the men bowed to each other. "May the heavens bless you and your family."

"And Liu Shang, a great philosopher and mystic from the East," said Majid.

"We are honored," said Liu Shang. They bowed to each other in a way that would honor any king.

"What joy to greet you all," said Gaspar. "Come let us tell Miriam of your arrival."

He then led us up the great staircase and into the great house.

# TREASURER

## Position of Fortune

My father came from a large and highly educated family. His father before him was a scholar of the stars and served the king in many respects—both in the preservation of historical knowledge as well as providing insight through the observation of our natural world. Majid's eldest brother and my namesake, Zebedeo, and their younger brother Gaspar, were exacting calculators who earned the distinction of high treasurers to the king.

Uncle Zebedeo's widow Miriam was sister to Gaspar and Majid by marriage. Miriam was the keeper of the residence and managed the private affairs of the Treasurer. She was largely responsible for maintaining Gaspar's home. Once a lovely and generous woman, Miriam had the unfortunate memory of the brutal death of her husband and the conflict surrounding it etched vividly in her mind. It also left a severity of her expression and a premature white to her hair. She was a disciplined but fair mistress and frequently reprimanded servants who took advantage of her kindness. One such servant was Hazar who had previously stolen Gaspar's golden bracelet. Gaspar being a forgiving and generous master gave Hazar the bracelet and allowed him to stay with the household staff. As a result, Miriam tried to watch the staff better and reprimand them when necessary. On the day we arrived, Miriam was instructing Hazar again.

"Everything around you belongs to the king Hazar and not his treasurer," scolded Miriam. "You are free man and not a bond slave and can leave at your leisure. So this begging and sneaking around must stop. Now, go and do your work or be gone with you altogether!"

Not noticing us, she turned around, slightly startled.

"Brothers! What a great joy to have you here," she said. "Come let us help remove the sand from your brow for we have prepared a great table for you and your friends."

Our house is yours," added Gaspar. "Please be welcome here."

We were led to the bathing gallery, a series of stone clad rooms with natural springs and waterfalls where the servants attended us. The color and fragrance of flowers were everywhere. Perfumed incense burned in small vessels perched on hanging platforms and cool fountains flowed from each corner of the airy rooms. Musicians played soft music in the background of this serenity. I enjoyed the hot mineral baths that our cousin's home provided and wanted to fall asleep in the process. But soon I was dressing for dinner. Miriam was in the kitchen coordinating the servants. As a good mistress, and a woman who took pleasure in entertaining the many guests that Gaspar frequently brought to the residence, she had the wine poured and a banquet suited for an army of men laid out on an expansive table. After our baths and prayers, we entered the dining room in a noble procession and were seated in grand style befitting persons well above our rank.

"Uncle, how is it that you are Treasurer to such a King?" I asked. "Is he a great warrior or a man of wisdom?"

"Neither, he's a horrible man," spoke Miriam softly as if the king were listening. "Herod has never stopped punishing anyone found in the company of his enemies."

"Please forgive my sister," said Gaspar. "She mourns the loss of her husband even now, these many years after his death."

"I speak of more than my own loss, my brother. Omar is without his father and it grieves us all. And Herod is to blame."

"Now sister," consoled Gaspar raising his brow.

"What? It is true," she whispered. "We live under the rule of a cruel man who abandoned his wife and child to marry the King's daughter."

"Some say that he was forced to marry her because he defeated a man who was trying to take the throne," added Gaspar softly. "It was a war we didn't think we'd win."

"Yet wars are won of the will," said Balthazar.

"It was the battle that killed my brother Zebedeo," added Majid for Liu Shang's benefit.

"Do not be fooled by Herod's cries for sympathy," Miriam declared. "He hates our people because many helped in the war. But the Emperor gave the throne right back to him and named him King of the Jews. He is nothing but a weak Roman puppet."

"A weak man with power is the worst combination," Majid replied.

"Agreed," added Balthazar.

"All the more reason to avoid him," said Liu Shang while snacking on small tidbits of the food before him.

"Our stay will not be long," I said. "We will leave as soon as we are able."

"Nonsense, keep silent dear sister," said Gaspar. "You're distressing our guests. Today, we shall eat and tell stories. Let us celebrate and make merry with our cousins and their friends. And Omar is eager to tell you all a tale."

Omar smiled widely. I sighed in resignation. He was a good boy with a dear heart but I knew Omar's tales and hoped my companions could tolerate them. There's often one family member apt to show off at large family gatherings that always embarrasses the others. Omar was such a person. I leaned over to my cousin so only he could hear.

"If you start telling stories, I'm going back to Tayma."

Omar gave me a puzzled expression then smiled widely. I was more than half-serious and did not return the smile.

"To our cousins who have graciously welcomed us!" said Majid raising his cup to toast.

"Praise be to God for our safe passage to Jerusalem!" Balthazar added.

"Trust in heaven . . .," Majid said rising signaling all of the men to rise.

Then we stood and replied.

"We are in this journey together, forever, always. Amen."

The music played while our meal began and we lounged around the banquet table among so many silken pillows that even my father was pleased. I wondered when we started saying that 'always Amen' statement but recalled that we have said it as long as I can remember. It must have been a family tradition as Gaspar and Balthazar recited it as well.

Later that evening we walked to the outer courtyard for tea and desert. The courtyard had within it a circular fire pit surrounded by a cushioned seating area and Gaspar motioned for us to rest. I knew this meant Omar would try to tell his silly tales and I dreaded every instant when the men enjoyed a silent pause in the conversation. The hookah sat beside Liu Shang who tried it for the first time. It was comical to see him cough at the taste of pungent Mediterranean tobacco. I couldn't see how any man enjoyed it. It was a horrible custom. Miriam brought a tray of tea and fig cakes out to the table.

"Tell us of your journey here," Gaspar inquired looking at me.

"We traveled a great distance through the wilderness and have survived an encounter with thieves and murderers;" I said smiling. "I wish there had been more."

"Zebedeo is keen on becoming a warrior priest like our friend Balthazar," Majid replied. "I only hope this old man can survive it."

"My father has little to occupy himself these days except to instruct me in all the ways that I am wrong," I said with a smile. "But in one thing, he has had great success. Cousins, we come to Jerusalem in search of the meaning of a great star. We believe it stands over a place where a new king is born. He is called the Messiah and the Deliverer."

Miriam arranged the tea on the table and served the men; keenly observing the conversation.

"What Zebedeo speaks is true," Majid added. "We have come to understand this as an omen that may bring the king of peace to all nations. We have observed strange movements in the heavens where one or more stars appear to have reversed course for a time and seem to completely stop in the sky."

"Zebedeo has mastered the star-guide he built and has detected the motion of these stars between one night and the next," said Balthazar.

"His calculations are correct," said Liu Shang. "I have checked them myself. They appear in the same manner described by the ancients of China."

"I am amazed beyond belief," said Gaspar. "As foretold by the prophets—a new king?"

Miriam was about to walk out of the room but stopped in her steps aghast.

"Brother, we cannot speak of this any further," Miriam whispered sternly. "If Herod discovers the purpose of your visit he will surely have us all killed. I beg you; do not speak of it any more!"

Hazar who had assisted Miriam with the desert was now hiding behind the curtains amidst the shadows and had overheard the conversation. The news of a child king seemed to disturb him greatly for he was not seen for the rest of the evening. On Miriam's notice of his absence, the other servants merely informed her that he must have been over-tired for he had risen very early that morning to prepare the residence for the arrival of the guests.

# TO THE DRESSMAKER
## ATTENTION TO DETAILS

I had spent the morning carving a small piece of wood in the shape of a star while sitting on the sunny rooftop near my uncle's home. The place had a great view of the city in many directions and the best view of the marketplace only a short distance away. While carving, I accidentally scratched my finger with the blade. The wound was genuinely produced from a distraction by the lovely girl I had seen a few days earlier. She walked with another girl into the marketplace, each of them carrying a small bundle of garments. A few paces away, one of the king's soldiers was talking to a small group of men. I could hear his voice rise and fall as if he were boasting of some military achievement. I had wondered if there were any skirmishes he might be discussing but dismissed the thought given the force and presence of the Roman legions that frequently passed through Jerusalem. Not hearing anything of significance, I went on with my carving, looking up every few moments to watch the beautiful girl make her way around the square.

"Good morning Rhia," a shop keeper said.

Rhia, her name suggests she is either Hebrew or Greek I thought. I had this painful curiosity about her. I could see that she was industrious given her circumstances—not only because she was a woman, but because she had the misfortune of a watchful eye of the lingering guards. And was I so different? It suddenly occurred to me. I watched as well. From what I could see under her head scarf, her hair was the same smooth cedar color I had first seen and her eyes were green as the new spring grass. She dressed rather plainly but looked very well given her station. If I had not watched her little brothers the other day, I would not have known that she was so poor.

It appeared that the two women had completed some sewing project for the dressmaker and were on their way to return the garments and obtain their wages. This guard, Severo as the men called him, walked up to the men in uniform and began boasting of his many courtly privileges from what I gathered. He and his men were deep in conversation as Rhia and her companion Mary passed.

"Rhia, when you get to the dressmaker tell him . . ." Mary paused. "Don't look now cousin, Severo and his men are here. We don't want him stealing from us again. Make haste; make haste."

The women tried to avoid Severo by looking the other way and quietly passing the group. They hid behind the merchant stands and walked behind men with large turbans as Severo was well into some story with his men. While I didn't want to admit it, Severo was certainly handsome, tall, and strong. And by having the King's favor, many women would be wise to enjoy his attention. But Rhia however, was not like other women.

"No finer goats in all of Judea and I will get the greatest price for the whole lot," they overhead Severo say.

"Best goats—ha!" Mary said with a chuckle. "He stole all of the finest goats from every local farmer. But what can a man do when no woman will have him?"

"Goats are much more willing to have such a master!" giggled Rhia. "Oh cousin Mary, I don't know how I would get on without you. You're the dearest thing next to the memory of my mother."

"Go quickly Rhia. The dressmaker wants those garments today."

"I will," Rhia replied.

The women kissed each other good-bye and Rhia stood watching and waving her cousin onward while Mary walked away. As Rhia collected herself and turned around to proceed to the dressmaker, she nearly bumped into the chest of Severo who towered over her with his men standing along side.

"And where are you off to my dear?" Severo asked.

Rhia was startled and flushed. She turned her eyes downward and away from his forceful gaze and instead, focused on the pebbles beneath her feet. She feared for her safety and recoiled from his attention.

"I'm on my way to wash our linens sir," she said softly while keeping her eyes locked on the pebbles below.

"The washing women are in the other direction," said Severo. "What is it you wash today?"

"Just linens my lord."

The guard grabbed the bundle she held and handed it to Severo. Severo smelled it.

"Hmm. A familiar fragrance," said Severo. He grabbed her arm and leaned into her ear.

I looked up from my carving and noticed Severo standing in the square holding Rhia by the arm in a threatening manner. I had a sudden urge to protect her and ran over several platforms to hear what was happening.

"In good time you will be one of my prized pets and your sweet linens will fill our bed," said Severo releasing her arm.

"Then I shall be a lucky woman," Rhia replied.

"Indeed," said Severo, delighted.

"Your love of your prized pets is known throughout the city," replied Rhia.

Severo failed to realize that Rhia had insulted him and fearing his understanding, she quickly walked away.

Having swiftly made my way across a couple of low rooftops, I was above Severo's group. As I stopped abruptly, I attempted to remain silent and regain my balance while Severo departed. But it was too late. My momentum put me off balance and I fell off the roof and into a hay cart making a loud noise as I came crashing down. When I regained my senses, Severo was long gone. Naturally, I was relieved. The cart owner however, an old woman, wasn't as pleased.

"Get out. Get out of here!" the old woman cried, swatting me with a broom.

I tried to get up, stumbling, and tripping over the cart, and myself.

"Sorry. Ouch. Oh! Sorry!" I moaned.

Several veiled ladies were gathered nearby and watched my current predicament. They were thoroughly entertained and merely laughed at me. I felt like the village idiot and I quickly retreated to my cousin's home.

Balthazar was finishing his morning prayers in the courtyard. I tried not to stare but his presence was compelling. His shoulders were broad and his arms were large and fierce. He had fought a few fights I suppose but I never heard him boast of any victories. He always seemed to focus on the path of honor and virtue. Right now, all I wanted was strength enough to wield a broadsword and carry a shield at the same time. Not that I could fight against Roman guards, but I was realizing that I might have spent too many days in the study of the heavens and too few days training in sword fighting.

"Zebedeo," Balthazar greeted. "You seem out of breath."

"I wanted to know if you have time to teach me something" I asked.

"What do you have in mind?" he said with a smile as if he already knew my interest.

After spending a few moments discussing my aims, Balthazar led me to the stables. He devised the most gruesome of physical tasks for me to master. He commanded that I climb bare metal chains fastened to the rafters, and soon thereafter had me lifting stacks of stones balanced on a lever, and moments later had me pulling a sled of grain sacks across the pathway. He helped me learn the art of evasion and modeled agility in combat using my sword, a spear, and improvising with whatever objects could be used to defend myself. Unfortunately, he would feel free to strike me upon the head, leg, or chest to point out my weaknesses. For days, Balthazar attempted to train me in the art of survival despite my intention to learn how to fight. And at the end of each session, feeling more beaten than victorious, I joined him in prayer.

"Oh heavenly and divine, one and true God," he began. "Lead us to the king, lead us to our destiny, and lead us to victory, we pray. Amen."

"What did you mean by destiny?" I asked.

"I believe that our purpose has been revealed Zebedeo," he replied. "And your destiny is to lead us to the new king."

"I can help guide us in a general direction Balthazar," I said. "But I am not a leader and certainly I am no expert in pinpointing the precise location of a *person* regardless of what the stars behold."

"Destiny, Zebedeo, is your purpose in this life and the one thing a man cannot choose," he replied. "It is a commission from God for you to use the talents he has given."

"So all of your speeches on free will were for your own personal amusement?"

"It's not like that Zebedeo," he replied. "A man accepts his destiny. He may choose to avoid it, but that would only lead to his ruin."

"I don't have that kind of ability Balthazar. And even if I did, God has better men for that job—like you for example; or my father. He can find the king Balthazar, not me."

"Do you think that your miraculous talent for not only seeing the coordinates of the stars better than any man alive but also for fashioning devices that can determine their exact course from one night to the next is coincidence—an accident?!"

"I can't. And besides, my father hates my inventions."

"And you think by gaining physical strength you will win the girl?"

"What are you talking about? You don't know anything."

"Maybe you should consider . . .," Balthazar replied.

"No!" I unwittingly shouted.

Walking away from Balthazar wasn't easy.

"I've had enough for today," I added in a calmer tone.

I had to leave and deal with my anger that had so instantly consumed my judgment and rationality. I loved Balthazar like a brother, a mentor, and a dear friend but his words pierced my soul and rang in my ears over and again. I knew that Majid was the one who could find the king if any of us could. And I could not face his anger, rebuke and disappointment when I failed to find the boy. It was not my calling. It was intended for another and Balthazar was sorely mistaken in believing in me. If he needed any confirmation of my failures, he could just ask my father.

# MERCY

## A Figure of Speech

The following morning the *Ma-ji* and company were called to Herod's Court to explain their business in Jerusalem. Needless to say, Hazar had sent a communiqué to someone in the palace and that someone was eager to investigate any rumor surrounding the arrival of a new king in the land. Majid, Balthazar, Gaspar, and Liu Shang were summoned to the palace by four of Herod's elite guards. They saw Omar and me, and decided we should come too. We were led to the King's waiting chamber. Though at first I was a little nervous, I let it pass. I had never met a king before, I thought.

Herod or, *King Herod the Great*, as he insisted, was a man of about sixty years and was appointed by Rome to rule over Jerusalem and its surrounding territory. His palace was magnificent, jeweled, golden, and opulent—befitting a ruler. In the rafters of his court, white doves sat like heavenly beings waiting in judgment. Through the high windows an angelic light pierced the room with a radiant serenity. In contrast, large black and golden bowls of fire flanked

43

Herod's oversized throne like an entrance to the gates of the underworld. Lavishly adorned noblemen, priests, scribes, advisors, and a few of Herod's elite guards—all gathered in the throne room to watch Herod's daily deliberations. These fearsome looking soldiers wore black capes and polished silver breastplates as bright as mirrors with the crest of Severo over their heart; a small shield ornamented with the head of a demon-like goat at its center. The entrance of the throne room was flanked by two large elite guards who stopped us at the doorway.

"You will bow down before The Great King of all Judea," the guard instructed.

Balthazar nodded and the guard eyed him with suspicion. We watched as Herod interviewed a poor young thief, beaten and bloodied by Herod's guards. I recognized him as the thirteen year old boy I saw in Jerusalem just days before. He was a thin-looking child. What kind of coward would beat such a boy? I thought.

"How is it that you came to possess fruit from my orchard boy?" Herod inquired.

"Master, I beg your mercy. I am Joshua. My father was killed and I am responsible for my brothers and sisters. I have offered my service to the King so that my family will not starve. I did not think such a great King would . . ."

Herod was shocked and for a moment left speechless by the directness and strength of the beaten boy. Any other waif in similar circumstances would have barely said a word. He should have known his place or so Herod would have thought. Severo appeared disturbed by the boy's candor and paced nervously. After a moment, he interrupted the boy's words.

"Enough!" said Severo. "The King grows weary of your mindless rambling. My Lord, what is your wish?"

"Your offense pains me more than your circumstance boy," Herod said coolly, regaining his composure. "I cannot have every peasant in the city stealing food from the palace, can I? What sort of gossip would follow?"

Two of the elite guards approached the child and the boy's hand was outstretched by a rope that bound him.

"No! I will repay you," cried Joshua. "Please, please, don't . . ." His voice was quenched by the flow of sobs and tears.

"Be grateful boy, for I am a generous and merciful King. Your life will be spared." Herod nodded to Severo. Severo motioned. An elite guard raised his blade towards the boy's hand.

I could not stand by silently. I tried to cry out in objection and pushed my way through my elders but was quickly silenced by Balthazar's firm grip on my arm and the other over my mouth. The young boy's hand was hacked-off and fell to the ground. He shrieked in anguish. The white doves scattered above and flew out the windows. I could barely contain myself and the rage inside me boiled like nothing I had felt before. A tear or two filled my eyes but I immediately fought them back. Herod motioned for us to approach as his soldiers took the boy and the severed hand away. The *Ma-ji* were released from the guards and motioned to step in front of Herod's throne.

This was not the king I had expected to meet. This was a villain, corrupted by the power that Rome had given him. What did the 'divine right of kings' really mean? I wondered if there was a Divine One at all. For who would allow such an injustice to befall that little boy? I was between rage and tears. I was between boyhood and manhood. And I wondered whether I would see such a day where I could put away my boyish feelings and rise up against this manner of tyranny—well, without getting myself or my friends killed, that is.

# COURTING HEROD

## On His Ground

I witnessed Herod's idea of mercy and I knew instantly what kind of man he was. Miriam's fears of his brutality were nothing next to the reality. We stood before this ruler on a blood-stained floor. For a moment I wondered how many souls had seeped through the cracks between each slab. And how many more would color the soil beneath the throne room. I quickly became present. It was our turn to answer.

"You are in the presence of Herod the Great, King of All Judea," announced a well dressed man.

He was either a High Priest or Grand Vizier. I didn't really care about his function in the royal court actually; they all looked like silly evil men to me.

"All must pay him homage," he added.

We knelt on one knee. Spattered blood surrounded us. The smell of it in the warm air was suffocating. The slaves wiped it up casually; smearing it with their blood-soaked rags. Omar was shaking in terror. Gaspar glared at him in the hope that he would stop. We rose.

"Who are you and what is your business here?" asked Herod.

"We are *Magupati*; priests and holy men who observe the heavens, my Lord," began Balthazar with a commanding voice and a princely bow. "We have traveled from the East these many months and have stopped here in your beautiful city of Jerusalem to pay homage and take rest. Our journey was ordained by the heavens as we seek He who is born King of the Jews whose star we have seen."

"I am the King of all Judea!" cried Herod. "What blasphemy do you bring here?"

Instantly, the elite guards lunged forward and drew weapons threatening the *Ma-ji's* lives. The crowd of nobles began whispering and mumbling to each other causing audible concern to the king. Balthazar was no fool but perhaps he didn't calculate that his words would have such great effect.

Quickly, Gaspar moved forward interjecting.

"My Lord, I believe that—what my noble guest means—according to some ancient prophesy, an antiquated myth perhaps—a star will appear as the new king is born."

Gaspar could barely speak the words, his voice cracking with anxiety, but he managed to continue.

"Perhaps it is you they mean to pay homage sire?"

"Silence!" ordered Herod. "Counselors?"

Several court priests gathered privately around Herod but it wasn't difficult for us to hear them. The noblemen and courtiers surrounding us were too interested to speak. Everyone waited and listened intently.

"Where is this Messiah born?" inquired Herod.

"Perhaps they speak of Bethlehem my Lord, the birthplace of King David, as foretold in the ancient text by the prophet Micah," said the first Counselor.

"Seventy-six generations have passed since the Creation my Lord," said the second Counselor. "And there is an ancient prophecy that the Messiah was to deliver Israel from its foreign rulers in the seventy-seventh generation."

"Is this true? Are you all in agreement that this is the proper hour that the Star-Prophesy might be fulfilled?"

"My Lord, we have observed the star," said the third Counselor. "But there is no cause for alarm. As you can see, it may refer to a time yet to come. And we don't know if the city the prophets speak of is in fact Bethlehem or some other place in Judea."

"I disagree my good King," said the second Counselor. "The star is like no other we have witnessed. It is visible both day and night. We must act now to secure your throne."

"This is a sensitive matter," said Herod.

"Your Majesty," interrupted Severo. "My men are ready to silence anyone who seeks claim to your throne. Let us destroy this false king and his *Ma-ji* before the people hear of it. And if we strike now, we will prevent any uprising and secure your place in history forever."

"Calm yourself Severo," said Herod. "All will be settled." Herod motioned the counselors away and turned to address the visitors.

"Well then, this is good news indeed," Herod began. "Tell me wise Zoroastrians to what city does your journey take you?"

"We are uncertain of the exact location my Lord," said Majid. "We know from our calculations and those of the great Master Liu Shang, that the place of the new king's birth should be near."

"Liu Shang?" said Herod.

"Yes my lord," Liu Shang said stepping forward with a bow.

"You are very far from home. Your presence in Judea shows us the seriousness of your search. A great search indeed," Herod said in a patronizing tone. "What say you Liu Shang? Where is this supposed king?"

The courtiers laughed in support of Herod but as the crowd quieted, Herod was answered.

"The heavens will lead us my lord," said Liu Shang.

Liu Shang was smart to avoid him but Herod did not appreciate the Chinese nobleman's vague reply. He wanted real answers, specifics, names, dates, places, and all the details attending this event, and as Miriam's account would prove, he'd stop at nothing to get what he wanted.

"Perhaps your long journey has taxed your—resources," said Herod. "I am a rich and generous king. Who among you is interested in my reward for finding the new king?"

There was a great commotion among the nobles in the room and Herod motioned for the crowd to stop. A sudden silence befell the room and not a single man made an answer.

"Treasurer?" demanded Herod.

"Yes my lord," said Gaspar.

"You will accompany the wise and noble *Ma-ji* on their journey to find the new king."

"But my Lord . . ."

"You needn't whine," interrupted Herod. "I will give you gold enough for your journey and your return. Go and search diligently for this child. And when you have found him, bring me word so that I too may pay him homage."

"Yes my Lord," replied Gaspar reluctantly.

I could see in Severo's eyes that he was not pleased. And though we did not set a date certain for our departure, he would be watching us. His guards would hope for our misstep. And we would have to be very cautious.

My eyes searched the room for one honorable face among them. But I could not find a single pair of eyes that did not side with the king. There were men aplenty and yet, not one man stood up against the king, let alone question his judgment. The blood not only soaked the floor but the souls of this crowd and their leader. I wondered what had happened to the boy Joshua and where had they taken him. Surely he would be tremendously weak, perhaps dead by now. His little brothers and sisters would suffer as well. Would there be no end to the evil in this place? Would this new king destroy this blood-soaked kingdom and replace it with one of peace as was promised? I was sickened. I was angry. But, in many ways like the boy who moments ago had been butchered, I felt weak and powerless against such men.

# POINT OF VIEW

## PLACE WITHOUT BOUNDS

I often climbed up to my cousin's roof in the late afternoon or before sleeping each night. The King Star had a particular elongated glow just as the light was changing between sunset and sunrise. It was a good time to watch the heavens during these quiet hours, for I was often left alone with my thoughts. And my daily strengthening exercises, which Balthazar had agreed to continue, left me wanting time alone with my thoughts before falling asleep from exhaustion.

One such early evening, I stood on the rooftop watching the movement of the stars while the villagers mingled in the distance below, packing up shop, readying for the next day, and sweeping up. This sweet evening began to sour as I saw the boy Joshua, weak and bandaged, delivered to his house. I stood up from my gazing spot and followed the men who carried him to the house of the poor family—the house of the beautiful girl Rhia. I walked along a few rooftops hoping to stay hidden. It was after all, just a short walk from my uncle's house and an easy distance. I feared the horror that his little brothers and sisters would encounter at the sight of him returning from Herod's court and wondered if there was something I could do.

The palace attendants carried him to the door and Rhia answered. At seeing her wounded brother, she turned and called to the children inside the house to help. The smaller children rushed out to carry Joshua into the house. I could only stand there, frozen, watching and wanting to help them, but what good could I offer? I was a stranger. Rhia was composed and her strength was much like what I saw in her young brother. I realized that I needed to move away, to stop invading this poor family's private trauma, but I could not. Rhia looked around and up. I gasped at being seen, and quickly moved away. Drawn to the sight of her, and compelled to investigate, I peered around the corner again. I saw that she had returned to the house but paused before closing the door for a moment as if to ask why this strange man was watching her from the rooftop.

"There you are Zebedeo." Balthazar's voice bellowed and startled me. I turned around and there he stood on the roof a few steps away. "If we are going to further our journey, you'll need an able mount," he added.

"What do you suggest?" I asked.

"Riding lessons," he answered with a grin.

I knew what this entailed but perhaps it would be easier than the earlier tasks Balthazar had devised for me. What might have been simple strength training for most would instead be a strength and character scalding for Balthazar—fire, water, earth, and wind or whatever it took to change a man. He had a strong belief that the tests we encountered in life were engineered by God—to purify our souls. Balthazar was the engineer in my mind. He had me balance a grain load normally carried by four men across a slender timber frame. And doubtless riding lessons would be much easier than carrying two baskets of stones hung on a pole across my shoulders while walking blindfolded over a narrow footing across a pool of muddy water. Riding lessons, I laughed. What fun Balthazar would make of it.

"What were you staring at down there?" he asked.

Nothing would escape his notice. Artful. Stealthy. Masterful warrior-priest.

"The boy." I replied. "From Herod's court."

He looked at me with that blank stare of displeased unbelief. He knew I was holding back.

"The girl," I huffed.

He smiled in satisfaction and placed his arm around my shoulder affectionately and walked me back to my uncle's house. I noticed the difference in his grasp. This time, it was not as heavy, nor as stifling. My strength was improving and my shape was becoming more like his.

That evening Balthazar instructed me on the ways of the ancient wise men. We lit some frankincense and sat together as he whispered a sweet prayer. And when he finished, he began.

"Close your eyes and clear your mind Zebedeo," he started, "and when your mind starts to wander and dream resist the temptation. Try to block out all things. Erase every image and every sound from your mind."

"I see white like the robes of the priests flowing in the breeze when they walk," I replied.

"That's a start," he answered. "Plain and white."

"And then what shall I see?" I asked.

"The light," he answered.

# LEVERAGE

## And Other Useful Purposes

I always saw Severo as an ambitious, bullying sort of man who felt that people's emotions were much better used as leverage than through the mere force of armor or weapons. As a Roman, he was very much an unwanted outsider, even through the eyes of his men who were local people who had been criminally captive or indentured servants. His position as an outsider was not enviable and perhaps it influenced his desire to better his lot in life. So he did what he could to survive and prosper. To prevent the men from building an alliance against him, he often pitted one man against another with the promise of freedom or a reward of gold, land, animals or wives.

A local villager came to my uncle Gaspar to complain that Severo and his men had represented themselves as the king's tax collectors. When some villagers refused to pay them, they were beaten. Severo became increasingly interested in one of their stories concerning a falling star they had witnessed. So this villager felt the king's treasurer should be advised. And so it happened that on one morning

Severo had asked a villager to his chamber to consult on the local terrain. They were looking at a map of Judea when two guards reported a strange event in the desert.

"What is it?" asked Severo of the intruders.

"My Captain," a guard named Malcaius said, "We have discovered something that warrants your direct attention."

Malcaius was a soldier as ambitious as Severo but perhaps craftier than his leader for he devised the falsehood of posing as tax collectors. After devising the ruse, the group immediately departed to investigate the area just outside the city. Severo, Malcaius and several other guards searched the shantytown near the city gates for witnesses to a strange event that had happened during the night. They went from house to house as representatives of the Treasurer to bully the frail and poor in search of more information. If anyone had information, the tax was forgiven. As word of the tax forgiveness grew, so did the story about the falling star.

"I saw a falling star the other night," said an old villager. "I was told by the tailor that its fire burned so hot that it melted the sand. A powerful stone is all that remains. It is said to be hidden in a cave somewhere and that is all I know."

Severo and the guards interviewed another villager who provided a slightly different account.

"No, no. Only a stone remains; clear like water," said a young man. "I heard from the farmer that an old man slept with it at night and it gave him great visions. But the stone was so powerful that it drove him insane."

As the stories grew, Severo became more interested. The stone could be a large jewel of value he thought—or better, it could have supernatural power. He and the guards continued the investigation.

"I heard that some children found some special rock. But they lost it while playing in the hills," said an old woman. "But you know how people exaggerate. It's just a metaphor and nothing to bother about."

Outside the shantytown, Severo gathered the small party of men.

"Whether myth or man, we will find this rock—this star stone," he said. "And I know exactly who will help us."

Severo and his men rode back to Jerusalem to prepare a scheme to find the stone.

"And they left us," said the villager to Gaspar. "I came directly to you. Should I have gone to the King?"

"I think the King is very busy and would want tax matters to come to his Treasurer," said Gaspar. "Do you know who Severo meant to speak with regarding the stone?"

"No sire. I can only imagine that he meant the men of the stars."

The man left and Gaspar and I discussed the stone. I pulled from my bag the long cylinder that I had fashioned. I explained that it was in want of an exceptional crystal to improve the view of the heavens—ideally to increase the clarity of the distant stars. Gaspar was intrigued.

"Do you think this is a glass that could be fashioned by a craftsman?" he inquired.

"My knowledge is limited in these matters uncle," I replied.

"If there is such a stone and it has powers, Severo is the last person who should have it," he said.

"How would a glass stone make a man powerful?" I asked.

"Severo is looking for some way to rise above his station Zebedeo," Gaspar explained. "The smallest accomplishment is all that is required in his mind because he lives in the shadow of another man and it eats at his soul."

"The senseless things that motivate men to conquer one another escape my understanding," I replied.

"You will understand soon enough the hearts of men Zebedeo," he replied. "Take care that it comes at a slow pace and be not so eager to rush into it lest you be seduced as well."

"A villain and a saint are easily distinguished," I said.

"In fable and folklore, to be sure." Gaspar replied. "But not so easily distinguished in life."

"And what of a crystal; might there be a glassmaker nearby?" I asked.

"Go to the marketplace," Gaspar replied. "Between the jeweler and the blacksmith there is a glass master. Seek him out and tell him that I have sent you."

"I shall," I replied. "Thank you uncle."

# JOSHUA

## AND A BED OF THORNS

The following day I stood at the doorstep of the poor children without any expectation of welcome but certain of my purpose. To escape the notice of the guard, I hooded myself in my darkest clothing thinking how cleverly I was disguised. Rhia opened the door and I boldly entered not knowing what I would encounter. As the only son in my family and losing my mother early in life, I had no experience with women or sisters. My inexperience made me feel awkward so I assumed that I should treat them with the same manner and indifference I would treat my cousin Omar. Although once I entered, I became nervous and felt awkward.

I inquired after the brother Joshua and was led to a sleeping alcove; the humble bedchamber that slept the entire household. Upon a small and somewhat thorny wooden frame with very little linen to cushion the load, rested the wounded boy. The place where his hand had been severed was now wrapped with dressing that, by the quality and detail, was clearly the work of one of the king's physicians.

"You are the man who gave us food," the boy croaked. His voice was dry and weak. His sister turned to offer him a sip of water from a small clay bowl.

"I am only sorry that it wasn't more," I replied. "Perhaps it would have saved your hand."

"You were in Herod's court?" the boy said with surprise looking at his sister. I had only hoped that my coming didn't shame him and make his misfortune worse.

"Yes, but I have brought you more this time so he cannot take the other."

"You are a generous master."

"What is your name boy?" I asked.

"Joshua. This is my sister Rhia. My father and mother were rug merchants here before . . . Sister, I have forgotten my manners, please bring our friend some tea."

"Yes of course," she replied and left the room.

"Forgive me master . . ."

"What ever for?"

"I must protect my sisters and brothers," said Joshua. "Yesterday was not the first time I met that man."

"The Captain of the Guard?" I asked.

"Yes" replied Joshua. "When I was very young my grandmother took all of us to pick olives in the grove while my mother and father worked. When we returned, I thought I heard my parents arguing. As we drew closer, I heard another man's voice. From his anger, I knew that my parents were in danger."

"Severo?" I asked but the boy merely nodded and continued.

"I heard him demand a payment," Joshua continued. "My father refused, 'payment for what?' he asked. Severo said that he protected all the merchants in his district and that my father must pay him or close the business. And I will never forget what my father said—he told Severo to fornicate with a goat!"

"Your father was a man of courage," I added.

"Severo was enraged," he continued. "He beat my father with the back of his fist and threw him across the room. The other men beat him as well. There were more words exchanged and then, he hurt my mother very badly."

"He is a monster," I said.

"My Grandmother tried desperately to hold onto me and keep my brother's and sister's eyes covered. Before I realized what had happened, my parents were dead. My Grandmother died not long after them." Joshua could not hold back the tears. "I'm sorry . . ."

"Your strength will return Joshua. Give it time," I said. "I will visit you again soon."

I left the room with a mind full of rage. As I headed for the door, I wondered how I should cast out this swine of a man who had violated all that this family held dear. The girl I now hoped to avoid stepped into my path. My feelings were fluctuating between rage and regard.

"Master, will you not stay for your tea?"

I nodded and reluctantly was led to the sofa. A small table and cushions were presented, which by the look of it, had been very lovely at one time. As I was seated, she brought the serving with great attention to detail and grace. Carefully, she placed a small brass tray on the table. On it rested a small tea cup and a small brass pot. A tiny violet flower had been placed next to the cup.

Slowly Rhia poured the hot tea. I watched as she pulled the honey stir from the pot and swirled it so as not to spill a drop. Her hands gestured as if to ask if I take honey. I nodded to decline.

I was struck by the contrast of abject poverty against Rhia's exquisite grace and beauty. I was speechless. Mesmerized by her movements and the perfume of her skin—I was overwhelmed.

Rhia's eyes looked down. I caught myself entranced and in realizing it, flushed in embarrassment. I reached for the tea, forgetting the steam I saw moments earlier and drank it. As it scorched my throat, I tried not to cry out adding further to my discomfort at this intimate setting.

Feeling uncomfortably warm, I rose quickly to depart. She smirked ever so slightly at my dismay and pressed her soft full lips together as if to fight a smile. We nodded to each other and I left.

As I returned to the streets, my thoughts turned to darkness. I wanted to kill that man. Severo was pure evil; a filthy being and a disgusting plague that should be wiped out of existence. The pain he caused this family was unforgivable. If I could seek him out, I'd expose him, I thought. But on walking further I knew I was powerless. It didn't matter if I were in Tayma or in this great city. I was a mere boy with righteous indignation and it tormented me. My uncle was right that soon enough I would understand the hearts of men. And I was no saint, but I clearly knew a villain.

I could hear my father's voice inside my head telling me that I needed to find the good beneath the evil and to hold onto it. At this moment, I realized that I could just as easily become the villain by destroying such a man and just as easily the man whom I call a villain could easily become a hero. Life pivots on an instant where we chose, of our own free will, where our destiny lies. I began to understand what Balthazar had been saying for all of those years. And for the first time I began to know my destiny.

# MOUNTED

## And Unbound

It was three days before we could settle on a horse that was neither too old nor too wild. Majid had approved our decision and Balthazar was using the horse to illustrate his lecture on Zoroastrian free will. The horse was a fine one—a deep dark sable with a white star upon his forehead. We settled on a grassy field that lay just outside of the city walls. The wheat grasses were uneven, brown and rutty—the time between harvest and new plantings, but they provided ample soft-landings should an inexperienced rider like me fall from his horse.

Balthazar explained how the harness and saddle were much different than a camel's and how best to properly maneuver my animal. After a few hours, I rode in the field with relative ease and the horse and I became more comfortable with each other. Balthazar waved approvingly from a distance as I galloped across the field that bordered an olive grove. Suddenly, something small quickly traversed my path, startling the horse. Before I knew it, I was thrown to the ground. As I gathered my wits and tried to open my eyes, the sun's glare blocked my view. I could make out a silhouette of a small child who ran away. As I rose, my head was ringing and I thought I heard the giggles of several small children. As I turned away from the sun, our eyes met. It was Rhia. She was standing with her siblings alongside. I initially thought that they had been playing in the orchards near the fields but on closer inspection I saw instead that she had been teaching her little brother and sister to sling a rock at a target—perhaps to defend themselves.

She saw my bewildered expression and laughed at me then turned to leave. I rose at once.

"Where do you go my lady?" I asked brushing the dust from my clothes.

"Seeing that you are well sir, we return home." Rhia said with a slight turn of her head. She smiled and continued away. I couldn't help asking after her. I wanted her to stay and knew it must be inappropriate. But I had to detain her if even for just a moment more. My heart was racing.

"And how is your brother?" I called after her. I felt like an idiot. She would surely think I was bothering her and her family, but it was the first thing that came to mind.

Rhia gave out a slight gasp and stopped in her tracks, turning toward me—her face was serious.

"He is still weak my lord but will recover soon," she said with her eyes down. "Thank you for inquiring," and she turned away, rushing the children home.

"I hope I did not offend you?" I asked but she made no answer and left toward the city.

Maybe I was rude. How was I supposed to know how to address her? This aggravated me to no end. But my thoughts turned to her smile. It didn't matter that the stars in heaven filled the sky that night. For in that moment, the only sparkle that I knew was the one deeply burning in my heart. Rhia—I could not forget her. Yet we would be leaving the city soon.

I turned back and saw Balthazar who had from a distance watched my fall. He had my horse by the reins. Well before he arrived, I searched his expression but found neither approval nor disapproval. It was his way. He could see things. He had visions. His dreams became reality and he spoke the truth that pierced men's souls. I feared to ask him about her and what would become of the children.

"Shall we ride together now Zebedeo?" he asked.

"Sure." I replied.

We set off riding together along the groves and as the horses galloped side by side, Balthazar looked at me and smiled. He seemed proud that I was a good student. But I should have known better. Balthazar was a master of playful deception and known for his innocent looking pranks and I had forgotten. Clearly, I was still a boy. He kept looking at me straight in the eyes, grinning widely. In all likelihood, his attention was deliberate so as to tempt me to continue to keep my eyes on him and not the road ahead. An olive tree branch had grown into the riding path and unbeknownst to me I had been heading right toward it for several paces. All the while, Balthazar had seen it coming. Within a few seconds I felt a painful blow to my chest and was thrown off of my horse. I hit the ground so hard that it knocked the air from my chest. For a second I felt like I could not breathe. That second ended and I felt in its place the pain and humiliation that comes from being tricked. I had been holding on to the reins but they had given way and my boot was caught; dragging me to the ground. Thankfully, after a moment my horse took pity on me and stopped dragging me around the wheat field.

"Grr", I grimaced.

I hated when he caught me off-guard. I could hear Balthazar's bellowing laugh as he galloped away toward Jerusalem. I struggled to remount the horse and finally pulled myself up and followed after him. It would be dark soon. And there was much to do before setting off toward Bethlehem.

# A PRIVATE WORD

## IN A DEN OF THIEVES

As much as I tried to get the blackheart out of my mind, the more he seemed to enter it from unsuspecting directions. A confirmation of Severo's dark nature came from my uncle Gaspar who related these events to me. And thankfully for my uncle, he had many secret allies in the palace. But the tale my uncle told started with an unexpected source—Hazar.

Hazar for many years was my uncle's first servant. The position brought with it distinction among his peers and in the community. Due to the discovery of a courtly scandal concerning Hazar and mounting pressure from the local noblemen, Gaspar was urged to either replace the servant with another or find him a young and beautiful woman to wed. It was believed by some that Hazar was having an affair with the King's wife and that he stole the golden bracelet from Gaspar in order to court her. But Gaspar had a kind and forgiving heart and simply gave him the piece. What matter? He had no care for such things. In letting Hazar stay on as a kitchen servant, Gaspar felt he was doing the charitable thing and many servants in the city received word of his goodness. Hazar was proud however, felt wronged at the demotion and soon sought revenge against his master. Penniless and powerless, Hazar sought the one person with whom he could barter—Severo. And information for money was a transaction Severo always entertained.

One evening Severo entered Herod's chamber to speak with him privately. Herod was clearly agitated and paced as he made plans to eliminate the threat of the new king.

"The moment the *Ma-ji* opened their little bearded mouths I knew they would disrupt my kingdom," said Herod. "But I cannot let your thirst for blood cause alarm among my allies. We must be discreet. And discretion has not been your strength Severo."

"I do not trust them. You've just given away a fortune in gold to the Treasurer. If I were him, I'd take your gold and never return."

"That's why I didn't give it to you Severo."

"Perhaps, sire. But the *Ma-ji* will not send word. We know that they journey soon and yet they would not disclose the location.

"We mustn't be hasty," replied Herod. "There are infants, suckling babes and innocent little ones who play in the courtyards." Herod sat down and placed his head in his hand.

"You think of your own child?" Severo asked.

"No you fool. I think of Rome! What will they say when they hear of this? I cannot do it."

"Yes my Lord. But I can."

"I know," Herod replied. "Give them a fortnight. If they do not return, they'll have my wrath to deal with."

"And my terms?" asked Severo.

"First, you must identify the child king and remove him quietly and bring him to me," Herod ordered.

"And if there is resistance?"

"Then you may use whatever quiet means necessary," the king replied.

"I understand."

"If you are successful, you will have the fortune you desire and I shall make you Ambassador to Rome." said Herod. "I will need a strong ally there after this."

"And the informant?" Severo asked.

"Give him the master's house," said Herod. "That is reward enough. And if he's lying, his master will return and cast him to the dogs."

"A fine outcome in either case," Severo replied.

"Discretion, Severo. You have your orders."

Severo left the king's chambers. As he marched the halls he planned his future. He would take a wife. He would sire an heir. His name would be held so high; so great, that it would dwarf the fame of his father. He would be Ambassador to Rome and at a younger age than his father. Steps outside Herod's chamber the informant Hazar waited impatiently with Malcaius, second in command.

"So long as this new king is a threat," said Severo approaching, "we will never make our fortunes."

"The king has accepted the information?" Malcaius asked.

"He has." Severo replied. "I must go now while Herod is agreeable to the terms."

"The *Ma-ji* will leave in less than three days." said Hazar.

"You are sure they depart for Bethlehem?" Severo asked.

"The final destination is still unknown," Hazar replied.

"Do not play with me servant," said Severo grabbing his arm.

"It is their course," said Hazar firmly pulling away. "But I know not where else they may search."

"If this king is born in Bethlehem then it's only fitting that the king's emissary should welcome him," said Severo. "Malcaius, gather the most vicious men in our company."

"When do we depart?" he replied.

"We have at least a fortnight. Tell them to make ready—sooner," said Severo, "much sooner."

# LADY IN WAITING

## WATER OF LIFE

My father had always been an early riser in Tayma. Each morning he would take a walk and I often accompanied him when I felt motivated to get up early. In Jerusalem however, we spent less time together. He busied himself with Gaspar's account of the recent problems with the Roman occupation and spent time discussing the heavens with Liu Shang and Balthazar. This provided me with time to move among the older men, stray off and tease my cousin Omar, or spend time exploring on my own. Exploring gave me the most satisfaction.

I made my way toward the olive grove on foot at sunrise. The day would be unseasonably warm—apparent by the smell of the morning dew evaporating from the wheat stalks remaining in the field. The fragrance of the clean air and the warm smell of the grasses created a surge of energy that pulsed within me. At first I walked but not long after I decided to pick up the pace and run along a path that bordered the grove. My boots were heavy but the fact that I had been strengthening my body, improved the way I felt.

It also helped that I wore the smaller of my two swords and a white tunic that covered some my chest and allowed my arms to move to the pace of my run. It was nothing fancy. And fancy out it the countryside was hardly necessary. My pulse quickened and the blood coursed through my veins. Beads of sweat drizzled their way down my forehead and back. It did not matter. My thoughts turned to the scenery. The olive trees, the greenery and the fresh air. Not far from here, I rode horses with Balthazar—lessons, I smiled to myself.

After a time, I heard the sound of water and turned down a path that led to a small creek. The water appeared fresh and cool. I walked closer and kneeled down to cup a handful for myself, splashing some of it in my face. It was quiet there and I decided to stay a while and rest upon a rock. I let the sun shine on my face and took in a deep breath.

The sound of a twig snapped behind me and due to Balthazar's training, within a matter of seconds I drew my sword and swiftly turned around.

"I am no threat to you sir," she said, frozen in place.

Rhia immediately realized the awkwardness of the situation. She was unescorted and I was not dressed for visitors. She wore a plain blue and gold gown likely made from expensive materials long ago. Although, she could wear a feed sack and look just as lovely, I thought. It became clear to me in that instant that this family was once wealthy and prosperous. And if the parents had been living now, the children would not suffer their present condition and she'd be wearing silken garments and ornamented veils like the other girls.

"My lady, I did not mean to threaten you." I said sheepishly. "I am sincerely sorry."

I saw that she held a small basket with what appeared to be small strips of cloth and little wooden pegs—an artistic project I presumed.

"I gather that I was sitting on your rock," I said with a smile.

"It is not my rock, sir," she replied sweetly. "But I do enjoy this place."

"And how does my lady spend her time here?"

"I recite psalms."

"Psalms?" I said with a laugh.

Having spent years in the study of science rather than the arts, my question was a direct result of my surprise. I soon realized that it smacked of unintentional mockery. I saw that the lady was disappointed and hoped to remedy my error by changing my tone at once and engaging her further.

"Please—sit," I asked.

"You depart?" she replied.

I could not tell from her tone whether it was her desire for me to leave or her desire for me to stay.

"I will depart if you wish it," I replied.

"It is proper sir," she said.

And she was right of course. Despite our innocent encounter, if anyone saw us together, she could be in dire trouble. I struggled. I was from a village where honor was much more important than formality. So I would honor the lady's request even though I hated the constraints of this kind of formality.

"Then I will do so. But recite for me a psalm that I may take it with me as I go."

"Very well," she said and set her basket upon the rock. "Let the wickedness of the wicked come to an end. Establish the just, for the righteous God tests the hearts and minds. The Lord is my shield who saves the upright in heart."

"It is lovely," I replied. "Do you have another?"

"I should be on my way," she insisted.

"I have overstayed my welcome," I replied. "I will go."

As I turned to leave, she started toward the rock and moved the basket to the ground. The place where she had stepped was muddy from the creek and gave way. She cried out and as I turned around, I saw that she was sitting on the ground holding her ankle.

"Are you alright?" I asked moving closer.

"I am fine," she replied. "The mud gave way."

"Let me help you."

I gently held her hand and steadied her as she tried to stand but she cried out again in pain.

"Your ankle is unwilling," I said. "May I please take a look to discern if it is damaged?"

She nodded and disclosed the ankle for examination.

"It appears sound but I think you will need to stay off of it for at least a day."

"Go and leave me here," she said. "I will rest a while and walk back a bit later."

"I'm afraid I cannot do that my lady," I replied. "God is not only testing our minds, he's testing our legs as well."

She gave me a consolating smile.

"I will deliver you to your brothers madam."

"But you have no horse—no cart," she said.

I did not answer. I handed her the basket and lifted her up.

"But I am a dusty maid," she protested.

"Yes madam," I answered with a smile.

The walk took a while and we were careful not to look at each other. She was light and even if she had been heavy, her beauty made it worth the task. I must have smelled awful, I thought and I hoped that she didn't notice. Soon we neared the courtyard outside her home and I placed her down at the doorway.

"Thank you sir," she said.

I placed her down next to me and waited as she steadied herself.

"I do have another psalm for you."

"I would enjoy hearing it," I replied.

"King David sang these words to the Lord," she began. "My spirit is overwhelmed within me and my heart within me is distressed. I spread out my hands to you. My soul longs for you like a thirsty land."

She had not moved away from me as she should and I knew not what to make of the words. I was silent—speechless. We stood in the courtyard and looked into each others eyes intently. Mary opened the door.

"I thought I heard your voice Rhia," said Mary.

"I fell and he carried me . . ." she began nervously.

"Never mind that, you had better come in now," Mary replied.

Mary helped Rhia in the house and quickly closed the door. It took me a moment to take it all in. The run in the morning sun, the cool water, and the chance meeting with Rhia all came vividly back to mind. Started to walk away. As I reminisced, it felt more like I had been the one who was carried away.

# MASTER'S MARK

## And the Faceless Token

I usually sleep soundly but that night I could not. A light from under the door disturbed me so much that I rolled over and pulled the blanket over my head. It was another night of fractured dreams and visions. They seemed to be coming more frequently now that we were settled in Jerusalem. Sometimes the dreams were clear and meaningful like the one where my father and I worked to gather water for a thousand thirsty people. But other dreams made little sense because all I recalled was the face of an animal—a lion, a lamb or a dove in flight with no other sign or symbol to interpret it.

It was during one of those odd animal dreams that I was awakened by a noise. I rose and wandered from my bed to my uncle's tally room. I watched silently as Gaspar melted the gold that Herod had given him.

"Zebedeo, what do you do at this hour?" said Gaspar. "Come in."

"I wonder why you've gone to such trouble uncle, to melt the gold only to make coins again." I said in a sleepy voice.

"The king will trace our every step and it will be measured by each place we leave his face," said Gaspar. He tossed me a coin containing Herod's image. "We will make the coins without a master and keep our passage a secret."

"Blank gold coins?" I replied.

"It is for our safety Zebedeo and for the safety of the new king," said Gaspar.

"How will you make so many coins?" I asked. "It will take all night."

"Indeed, I have worked many nights. Go and sleep."

"No. I will work too. But you must help me do one thing."

We started by adding more candlelight and I explained how I needed to use some of the gold coin. My explanation was a bit cryptic, but Gaspar understood that I was protecting someone. He was a good uncle and trusted me; leaving me to fill in whatever details I wanted without questioning my motives.

As we worked, he demonstrated the process of melting the coins in the metal cup over the fire. We set up the process in small quantities allowing them to cool in the wood molds he had made. Hundreds of tiny coins filled mountains of trays. I followed his instruction carefully, trying not to spill a single drop of the liquid wealth. I wondered how we would get through the mountains of coins in only a few hours that remained in the night.

My thoughts were turned toward a woman, and I was quickly and effortlessly falling in love with her. The hours rushed by and somehow, though my mind was completely and effortlessly preoccupied, I made no mistake in my tasks. As we watched the sun rising, we were cleaning up the counting room, tidying the floor and clearing the tables of any wasted gold flake, drops or scraps. We would leave the tables as they were normally kept—clean, orderly, and without a trace of what we had begun.

Gaspar knew that Herod would expect us to litter our path with the gold he had provided. He also had deliberately given Herod the impression that he was too timid and weak to challenge his master. In fact, his entire reputation was built on his honesty and humility to the King. No one would think of him differently. Herod also believed that by providing so much gold, Gaspar would not have time enough to do anything but take it and go; leading him straight to the new king. One thing we all knew was that Herod would kill the innocent child to ensure his control over Judea. And with Severo commanding his legion of elites, no man could stand in his way.

While Gaspar finished, I found some black liquid that he used to write on his tally sheets.

"Gaspar?"

"What is it?"

"Would you mind if I take some of your black writing liquid?"

"This? Yes of course," Gaspar replied. "It is very powerful. You need only a little."

He poured the fluid carefully into a small vial, sealed it and gave it to me.

"What will you need this for?"

"I have an important message to deliver," I replied.

# SHADOW OF
# A MAN
## FRACTION OF A SON

It wasn't easy for Severo to grow up in the shadow of his father. Quintus Marcus Severo was a General of the Praetorian Guard and a close friend and military advisor to the Emperor. Quintus, as he was called by his friends, had an illustrious career that was made all the more noteworthy because he was from the land of the Hellenes and not from Rome. Not long ago, the high positions of the Roman Government were reserved for the men of noble and aristocratic families of Roman heritage. The trend in the Empire now, moved towards a society where one's knowledge, skill and personal alliances were as important as any family connection. Quintus also accrued many accomplishments in military and political spheres particularly due to his strategic intelligence and his unusually good looks. He thwarted the Hebrew revolts, was the commander of the prestigious Aegean Fleet, and was promoted to the level of a Praetorian Prefect by the age of twenty two. By age thirty he had become the de facto Ambassador to Egypt. His beauty and early success contributed to his vanity. And his vanity fueled his lust for control which consumed him and left him with few, if any, friends.

Quintus was neither good nor wholly evil, he was merely a man corrupted by power. In his frustration, he beat his wife, he beat his sons, and he beat his servants. He drank heavily and would challenge men to bare knuckle fights that led many to their graves. Not long after his fortieth birthday, a rare and crippling illness confined him to bed. The cancer consumed his bones and knotted his joints. His beauty was forever lost and with it his power faded. After his wife died in an accident and his servants fled, there was no one to care for him in Rome. Antonius Brutus Severo, the only surviving son, brought his father to his home in Jerusalem with the thought that his own alliance with King Herod would provide him access to the royal physicians.

While much of his glory had faded away, Quintus had become no more than a strong willed and an insensitive old man. The disease had taken over much of his body. The lines on his face, the whiteness of his hair, and the twisted knots that shaped his form, caused him tremendous and frequent pain not only in his person, but to his pride. Despite the degradation, despite the verbal and emotional abuse he endured, despite the lowliness of the tasks of caring for his dying father, Severo was there for Quintus. Each day he fed his father, dressed him, groomed him, and in the evening prepared his supper and drew his bath.

"Why do you always make the water so cold Severo?" said Quintus. "Is it really so difficult to provide an old man with a hot bath?"

"I am sorry father," Severo replied. "Shall I go and get some water from the kettle on the fire?"

"Why, so you can boil me to death?" Quintus shouted.

"I will do whatever pleases you."

"You have never pleased me," the old man answered. "Your mere presence disappoints."

"I will leave you to your bath then father," said Severo.

"There has always been a sad lack of determination in you boy."

Severo was losing his patience. He turned back to his father and watched as the steam from the bath danced in the air; mirroring the rising heated feelings for his father.

"I recall a letter you once sent me from the battlefield. It contained a list of merits you wanted in your sons: wisdom, courage, determination, and above all else, excellence."

"It was during the campaign at sea you oaf, not a battlefield," Quintus interrupted.

"I knew then that I could never live up to your expectations," said Severo. "I had other merits such as ambition and industriousness. But you cared nothing for my merits. Then, as it is now, you act as if I mean nothing to you."

"My life has been a battle on many fronts," said Quintus. "But what we make of it is our own choosing. Why should you receive better favor than anyone else?"

"I have searched the heavens for a way to make you love me father," he replied. "I have hoped beyond all hope for one kind word or one gesture of affection from you. What is it that you hate in me so much?"

"You do not strive for excellence Severo," he replied.

"I have only wanted to live up to your expectations even in the smallest measure."

"Do not try. You are destined to fail."

# DESERT FLOWER

## USEFUL BLOOMS

In the days that followed we had purchased supplies in the marketplace for our continued travel. As there would be some uncertainty about where the king star might lead us, we wanted to be sure we had ample provision for the animals and that the food and water for us would be as plentiful as possible considering that we were adding few more to our party. Gaspar was an experienced traveler in his youth, but had not traveled far in many years. Miriam and Omar had never traveled beyond the few small towns that surrounded Jerusalem and neither seemed enthusiastic about leaving the comforts of the grand house they had known for so long.

I'm not sure why it took so much time for them to gather and pack. Balthazar, Liu Shang and I had provisions prepared in one afternoon. While the others were occupying themselves with which robe to wear or which golden hairpiece would be best before the new king, Omar and I spent time wandering about the city on foot. I would try to locate the glassmaker but was distracted by the other, more masculine wares. There were many interesting new swords to inspect and the blacksmith was proud to show me a new jeweled handle he had fashioned on a long sword. I thought it was foolish to have such a weapon I admitted to his dismay. It was far too heavy to use when quickness and agility were most often required. Omar preferred throwing knives.

"Hey, look at these," chirped Omar.

"Those would be good," I replied. "But you would need to be really close to the villain."

"Eww. Right. What about this one?" he said picking up the metal tipped razor sharp spear."

"That one will travel sixty feet and is decidedly accurate," said the blacksmith.

"How much?" Omar asked.

"Omar . . ." I warned.

"Seriously," he said looking at the blacksmith, "how much?"

"I cannot negotiate that one," he said, "Three gold minimum."

Thankfully, nearly everything was out of Omar's price range. I would have hated to explain his purchase to our elders. The blacksmith began to tell Omar a story about how his father's father once cut off a man's arm with only a small dull throwing knife. I quickly interrupted the smith's story. Omar had spent most of the previous evening telling the men from the east his absurd stories and I didn't want to be embarrassed again tonight when he recounted this man's ordeal. It was time to move on.

We passed a jeweler, a potter, and a flower peddler. But there was no sign of a glassmaker and I had hoped to find a crystal for my star-guide. The perfume of the incense nearby was pleasant and perhaps a bit distracting from my true purpose of finding a glassmaker. Perhaps the warmth of the air and all of these luxuries mixed together could explain the feeling that came over me in that moment. A few paces from me a young man had lovingly clasped a jeweled bracelet on his lady's wrist. She looked so happy. I was compelled with the desire to buy something for Rhia—something to show my affection, to show that I was thinking of her, and express my feelings. I told Omar to go ahead home without me. I needed some time to look over a few things. He did as I asked. I went to examine the small polished beads presented by one merchant and was approached by several others wanting to sell me oils, elixirs, and silks. I became overwhelmed by the cacophony of voices. And alas, I caught myself. A gift would be completely awkward. What was I thinking? Rhia would think me a complete fool. Turning away from all the confusion of the marketplace and the competing merchants, I pressed on and headed back toward my cousin's home.

It didn't take long before I was lost in my thoughts again. I was attempting to decide the best route for the journey and wondered how the horse would manage the task particularly since I only rode a camel on trips of this distance. I woke from my day dream and found myself in front of Joshua and Rhia's home. Rhia was standing precisely before me watering a potted flower plant on the walled courtyard that faced the pathway. Apparently she also was deep in thought and we had startled each other at the same time.

"Forgive me my lady," I said with a laugh.

She smiled and turned her eyes down in humility.

"It is a very fine day, is it not?" I inquired not knowing what else to say.

"Sir, you know that I cannot speak with you without my brother present." she replied.

"Then perhaps we should call him."

"He is resting," said Rhia softly; her eyes rising to meet mine. I moved closer and nearly touched her hand which rested on the low wall that separated the courtyard from the pathway.

"That is unfortunate because I just saw the fattest pig in the marketplace and I wanted to ask him if it he too thought that it resembled the Captain of the Guard."

Rhia let out a laugh and in that moment I felt the intensity of my affection. This was my paradise; to be in her company. It was all that mattered.

"Your ankle is well I see."

"Indeed, very well thank you," she replied.

Mary walked up to the house and entered the courtyard through a low gate. She gave me a nod whispered into her cousin's ear. Rhia nodded to me then departed into the house.

"Forgive my manners sir, but you must leave," said Mary in a maternal tone. "If Severo sees your attention to my cousin, he will kill you and hurt the children."

"Why would he—?" I asked. Mary understood my question before I could ask and moved toward the door to step inside.

"He intends to marry her," she said as she closed the door.

That was more than enough to make me sick. I felt as if my bowels had been severed and pulled from my groin. In an instant my paradise was lost and the hollowness I now felt was mortifying. Was my happiness to be gone forever at the hands of the man who would only cause more pain and suffering to this family? This could not be.

I thought I had set aside my anger for this villain but all of those feelings came rushing to the forefront of my mind.

My blood boiled. My brow sweat. I stomped off furiously and deliberately. As I returned to my uncle's residence, I saw that things were nearly ready for our departure. It was clear that I had to act immediately. I informed the servants that I needed a special bath, one that we use for purification and before deep prayer, fasting and meditation. While it was not the usual time for bathing, let alone the time for ritual purification, they did as I asked. I bathed and retreated to a solitary room and began.

"Oh heavenly and most high Lord

We embark soon to find the child king.

And you have commissioned us to serve in this manner.

I walk with your Holy *Ma-ji* on this journey and will do as you command.

May your virtue shield them.

May their words be true.

May their swords be as your Word and cut through all unrighteousness."

I knew that I shouldn't pray for my own selfish desires, but there was heaviness on my heart and I could not help myself. I needed some, however small, assurance that she would be free from the clutches of an unworthy and despicable man. I prayed and prayed again. And when I was exhausted, I prayed a bit more.

"Please oh sacred and Holy Father

I lift up Your daughter of Israel

She is fair and she is righteous

A godly woman by all who know her

Please deliver Your daughter from evil

Please deliver her brethren from harm

And in return, I shall teach my sons to honor You

A symbol of my faith shall I wear openly

And I shall surrender to You my destiny
And in Your name shall I cast down your enemies
For on this day I ask for a new life
I ask to be reborn in spirit and mind
Please sacred and Holy Father, for a miracle I pray
Deliver us from this evil and
Deliver unto us the king of peace. Amen."

# LADDER OF HOPE

## LEAD US TO SALVATION

The sun was setting and outside Gaspar's house I joined the men to depart. It was time to follow Majid who would lead us to the Great Star and the new king. The attendants of the *Ma-ji* were helping everyone get mounted and servants of the house made the final provisions for our meals as we planned to depart Jerusalem. It appeared as I sensed, that we could never return. And if we disobeyed Herod and did not return with news of the king, we would be slaughtered just like the many souls who bled upon his throne room floor.

Our party was joined by Gaspar, Miriam and Omar. Omar mounted my camel and I rode alongside Balthazar. My horse, which I had named Midnight, was well equipped for the journey and seemed brave enough for the trip like Eclipse—well, maybe. I did not forget the fact that a group of small children startled him in the wheat field just days ago. As our party assembled for the journey, I mounted Midnight and turned to leave in another direction. I had one final task to complete in Jerusalem and started away.

"Zebedeo, where are you going? We depart soon," shouted Majid.

"I will meet you at the city gate," I said turning on Midnight.

I was cloaked in a dark hooded cape; my face hidden from sight and I rode through the city quickly making my way toward Joshua's house. This was one of the most important things I had to do in all of my life. I would need to be unfaltering in delivering my message. I could not let my feelings for the girl get in the way. If I did, Severo would destroy them all. He would force her to marry him. He would kill the others.

I slowed Midnight and paused in the marketplace—a flower peddler had left a few desert roses in a pot to be discarded so I lifted them up. When I arrived at the house, I could not bring myself to give the flowers to Rhia, so I set them at the doorway. I took a deep breath and knocked. Rhia opened the door and I entered. As I removed my hood, my eyes could not disguise my adoration for her and my heart began to race. I had no idea what to expect but she seemed glad to see me too. The moment was quickly interrupted by Joshua who entered the room.

"You have come again to visit."

"Yes. I bring a gift to help lessen your suffering."

I handed Joshua a heavy bag of gold coins.

"Take your family and leave this place," I continued. "Tell no one of this visit. Tell no one of this gift. Your wealth and your lives will be in danger if you stay."

"We must leave tonight?" said Joshua.

"At once," said I. "You have not a moment to waste."

"I understand," he said softly. "He is coming for us."

"Do not wait," I insisted. "Take your brothers and sisters and go."

"Thank you brother," cried Joshua. "May God bless you and your family, now and forever."

I was glad this went well and Joshua quickly accepted my gift and my orders. He understood the threat on his family's life was imminent. He was now equipped to do something to save them. But the moment passed too quickly. I was unable to say my farewell to Rhia. I felt like a confused boy, struggling to be a man. Mostly I felt like an idiot. I turned to leave. Rhia followed me to the door. But at the last moment, I turned to her.

"Do you read?" I asked as my heart raced in fear.

"Yes, a little," she replied.

"Of course," I recalled with a smile. "Psalms."

I placed a small scrolled note in her hand—bound with a thin leather cord and ornamented with the small wooden star I had carved.

"Follow these instructions and your family will be safe." I said sharply. "You must keep this information to yourself and your brother. Leave as soon as it is dark. Do you understand?!"

Rhia was visibly upset by the apparent anger in my tone and my rude departure.

"Why do you leave so soon?" she asked as her voice shuddered with emotion.

I felt my face become heated with nervousness. It tore me apart to leave her but I knew she would be in danger if I wasn't strong. It was obvious that Severo had more painful plans for this family and I couldn't let that happen.

"Do you understand?!" I repeated. She began to weep.

"Yes, yes," she cried.

I touched her gently on the arms and lowered my voice.

"You must escape this place. Leave tonight."

I started for the door, opened it and turned back to look at the young woman I had wounded. She had done nothing but serve others and show kindness. I was the brute. Hopefully, my cruelty would save her life. I might never see her again but I would be comforted to know her family escaped the cruelty of this place. She followed me to the door.

"Who may we remember in our prayers this night?" she asked resigned to this end.

My expression softened and I touched the tear on her cheek. I moved my fingers down to her chin, raising it and our eyes met. My heart was racing. I almost moved to kiss her full and beautiful lips but stopped myself before I forgot that I needed to get her away from Severo. There wasn't any time to delay. They had to leave now.

"The message contains all the information you need—and more, if you wish it." I replied.

I moved away to depart.

"And your name?" she asked softly touching my sleeve.

"My name is Zebedeo. It means 'servant of God.' Let your praise be to Him."

I left the house and closed the door behind me. Staring down at the flowers, I placed them at the threshold. I hesitated to leave and looked longingly at the door, wanting to go back and speak to her. I would confess, perhaps to my shame, that I loved her; my heart was hers. My soul was agitated by a passion that I had never before experienced.

But I could not—I ached as my selfish desires waged war with my inexperience. And right now she must leave Jerusalem and be safe. And I must continue on my journey. As I turned to leave, the face of the goat crest—the villain's crest, met my gaze. And as I slowly looked up, Malcaius' menacing eyes peered down at me.

"Going somewhere? Malcaius asked.

I was taken by surprise and had nothing to say. Three elite guards accompanied him and I was instantly seized by two of them.

"Lock him up," replied Malcaius as he walked over to examine the pot of roses.

I started to speak, to shout at him in distraction as I saw him moving toward the doorway, but the third guard hit me in the stomach and threw me in a cart. As they drove me away, I could see Malcaius enter the house with the flowers I had intended for Rhia. I heard Malcaius' voice followed by Rhia's scream. As the cart led me away, I tried to cry out, to object, to call for help—anything, but one or more of the guards began kicking me and I lost sight of my surroundings. I heard the sound of the flower pot crashing to the floor, echoing the sound of my world crashing down around me.

# CAPTIVE
## AND CRIMINAL

It was a clear Jerusalem night. I was supposed to meet our caravan at the gate hours ago. Instead, at the hands of Severo's men I was imprisoned in a cold hard holding cell looking out at the stars between the silvery columns that fenced my window. At least the King Star still stood high in the sky. It gave me hope. I thought of my prayers and the Psalms of King David that Rhia had recited. David was an ordinary boy who became a great man in a great hour. And then sadly, I realized that I was nothing like him. Severo approached my cell and a guard opened the door. The interrogation began.

"What were you doing lurking around the streets like a bandit?"

"I am the son of the *Ma-ji*. We follow the star and I am dressed for travel."

"Ah, yes, you were in Herod's court. And where is it that you travel?" asked Severo.

I looked at him with suspicion and knew that nothing good would come of my conversation. Even if I told him the truth, he'd probably kill me.

"I only mean to assist you boy." he continued. "Although I am a Roman, I have lived here many years and know all the best roads to any city in any direction."

Severo was trying to win me over—convince me that we were friends, or at least that I could trust him with information. But I had not only heard of his misdeeds, but watched him in court and in the marketplace. He was the kind of man you should avoid or kill. There was no middle ground.

"We go wherever the star leads; and that is the road we take," I answered.

"You are very knowledgeable about the stars, yes?"

Despite thinking he was subtle, Severo clearly had an agenda—obvious to anyone with half a mind.

"Yes," I replied.

"A report has reached me of an alarming nature. A falling star has been seen. Do you know of it?"

"No."

"Funny that you are a man of the stars yet you have not noticed one that has fallen?" Severo said suspiciously.

Perhaps he was cleverer than I thought.

"At present, I watch the stars that are still," I said with the most sincere tone I could muster.

Severo paused in his pacing, and turned to look over his shoulder at me; uncertain of the meaning of my remark.

"Indeed, men of many professions like to curse when anything new or unexpected makes their job more difficult. Would you not agree?" he continued.

I shrugged.

"Do you speak from your own experience?" I asked.

Severo grew impatient and his tone became hostile.

"Boy, are you aware of who I am? I have the power to end your life this instant if I choose it!"

Severo began pacing about the cell stopping before me.

"Now answer my question," he continued. "Do you know anyone who has seen visions from looking into the stone of a falling star?"

"I am too old to play with rocks my lord; even if they fall from the sky."

Severo slashed me across the face with his gauntlet. Blood spattered like painted lines and dots along the stone-laid floor. I was dizzy. A vision of the throne room consumed my mind and in the haziness, I recalled the slaves of Herod's court in black hooded robes on hands and knees making swirls on the pavement with their blood-soaked rags. One by one the robed bodies turned toward me. Their pale ghoulish faces looked me in the eye—they were not of this world. They were straight from the fires of the damned.

"Impudent boy," he murmured in disgust.

By now, I had regained my wits. Severo departed and the guard closed the door. I was left alone with my wounds and my rage. From across the hall I could see that Kahim the thief captain, speckled with berry stains and camel manure, was staring at me and giggling from his cell. This was truly humiliating. Not only was I in the company of such filth, but I had become the brunt of another man's joke.

Moments later, Omar appeared peeping through the barred window. The bars were hinged with a small lock securing it in place.

"Psst. Cousin, we thought you'd left Jerusalem without us," Omar chirped with a smile.

"Can you get me out of here?" I asked but as I looked up Omar had disappeared.

"Omar, where are you?" I continued.

Omar appeared again through the window.

"I will get you out if you let me tell you a funny story," he teased.

"Blast it Omar! Get Balthazar."

Omar disappeared again and Balthazar peered through the window.

"Mind your patience Zebedeo," Balthazar replied. "We're working on it."

"It used to be a stable," Gaspar instructed. "The gate covers the hay window. We could try to pick the lock with your knife."

"I think I know what to do," said Liu Shang.

Majid peered through the window and saw that I was injured. That was the last thing I needed—my father's worry.

"Zebedeo! What trouble have you got us into now?" Majid blurted. "You will have us all killed by that madman."

"Shh Majid," Balthazar cautioned. "Keep your voice down. We almost have it."

I could do nothing but shrink back in shame which only added to my rage and encouraged Kahim to snicker at me again. Thankfully Midnight had returned to Gaspar's residence or they wouldn't have thought to look for me so soon. Within moments, Liu Shang poured a solution over the lock. Balthazar covered it with a cloth and then pulled it open; twisting the metal as it gave way. Kahim stopped smiling. Quietly, the men lifted me out of the cell window and Balthazar tossed Kahim some gold coins to keep him silent. I counted my blessings and quickly mounted Midnight. Within a few moments we were clear of any guards and rode to meet the caravan. Outside the gates of the Holy City, the *Ma-ji* quickly came together and began to move onward.

"Majid," said Balthazar in a commanding tone, "I think it is time we let Zebedeo lead us to the child king."

"We have no time for that Balthazar," Majid replied. "We must get away from this place before the guards discover that a prisoner is missing."

"Just think how angry that man will be," Liu Shang added.

"Let us go in any direction, I do not care to tarry," said Majid motioning his camel to advance.

"No, Majid" Balthazar ordered and grabbing the camel's reins. "Zebedeo has been anointed. You know this to be true and saw it in your own dreams."

Everyone dismounted. Majid's countenance changed. His stubbornness faded. He turned his animal around and rejoined the group.

"Zebedeo?" questioned Majid. "Do you mean the young man who just angered the head of the elite guard and put all of our lives in jeopardy?"

I lowered my eyes and could not bear to hear any more of my father's disappointment. But Balthazar stood steady in his countenance. He was not asking my father to yield, he was telling him to do so. Majid laughed a full belly laugh and smiled at us all.

"Stop speaking of me as if I weren't here!" I demanded. The men grew silent.

"I need to find someone. I need to make sure that she's safe."

"You cannot go back Zebedeo," replied Balthazar.

"Just watch me," I said attempting to move past them.

Balthazar snatched my arm with a grip so powerful that it made no difference that I had become much stronger—his strength was no match for mine.

"You cannot," he soothed "Because she is gone."

"What do you mean, she's gone," I implored.

"We must continue," Balthazar insisted.

He released my arm and I shrugged away as if I had actually escaped. We both knew better. I reluctantly mounted Midnight and the men followed and mounted their camels.

"We shall follow you Zebedeo," my father replied, "if you choose to lead us to our doom or to the Deliverer. I for one hope it is the latter, for we are in dire need of him."

What was this madness between us? And was my father joking? He never let anyone else lead the way. I pulled out the star-guide from my bag and made a few more observations. I determined our course and led our party.

We traveled a few hours into the night then stopped to water the animals. I used my cousin's black liquid and painted a small inscription on my cheek, the new inscription that I had promised in my prayers. A symbol of the *Ma-ji* I decided. The design was made up of a small version of the king star and a symbol for our profession in my home language.

It was a bold statement and I was risking another humiliation. But again, I wanted to do things my own way now. I would stop doubting myself. I would need strength and courage if I were to go back and find Rhia. I would need to resolve all that had happened. I would find out what became of the children. I feared for them. I feared for us.

Severo returned to the prison hours later. There were no words for the level of his anger. He appeared calm. But as he walked out of the empty cell, he pulled a dagger from his glove and cut down in cold blood the man who was posted to guard the prisoners. Malcaius approached him.

"Where have you been?" Severo demanded.

"I was knocked unconscious," my lord.

Malcaius had a large bloodied gash over his brow.

"What happened?" replied Severo.

"Just a silly flower pot," said Malcaius "knocked from a window sill."

"Get that cleaned up," Severo demanded. "We meet with Herod soon."

# CUT SHORT

## A MAN ON FIRE

After losing me in an inexplicable prison break, Severo came home in an angry uproar. He stomped into the house, broke a bottle while reaching for some strong drink and said nothing to Quintus who was sitting next to the hearth. Quintus appeared unusually weak and tired. And Severo did not attend to him as he usually did but poured himself a large serving of spirits, drank the entire portion, then poured himself another.

"You look especially foul this evening," said Quintus, still staring into the fire.

"Look what I come home to," replied Severo moving toward him.

"And I am equally rewarded," Quintus replied.

"A prisoner escaped today."

"Ha! Failure again?" Quintus chirped. "Let me guess, your prisoner was an infamous thief?"

"Enough," Severo demanded.

"The butcher of Babylon?" mocked the old man.

"Silence!"

"It is of little consequence," Quintus replied.

"You enjoy taunting me father, even now?"

"Everything you touch Severo will wither and fade away. You are cursed."

"You are wrong father," shouted Severo. "I have five thousand gold waiting and a position as Ambassador to Rome."

"It will be snatched from your hand, just like your bride."

"What are you blathering about?!"

Quintus said nothing but gave Severo a sinister smile.

"Tell me this instant! What has become of the girl?"

"The maid saw her and the children leave hours ago," Quintus replied. "You are a cursed man."

"Liar!" shouted Severo in an uncontrollable rage.

Quintus merely laughed at him. Severo became dizzy from his father's laughter and the room began to spin. He threw the bottle of spirits into the fire. And like the fire blazing in front of them, Severo could no longer be contained. He threw the old man off of the chair. But the man could not defend himself and fell beside the embers. The blanket that covered him quickly caught fire and in an instant the old man was consumed by it. Severo was beside himself in horror. On the one hand he wanted to stop the blaze but a vile and unearthly wickedness consumed his soul for in this instant all the hate he beheld for his father was now unleashed on the old man. The cruelty he had endured for years would come to an end this night. He wondered whether the murder of his oppressor made him a greater man, or if he had merely become his proxy.

Severo gathered his men and made their way to the house of the poor children. When they arrived, the house was dark and quiet. Malcaius kicked-in the door and Severo entered. Just behind the door lay the broken the flower pot that Rhia had thrown upon Malcaius' head, knocking him out cold and giving the children enough time to grab what few treasures they had before they fled the city. Malcaius was sure to step in front of the fragments so that Severo would not see them.

"It appears they have left, my lord," said Malcaius.

"Find them," replied Severo.

"And what next?" Malcaius asked.

"Burn it," replied Severo. "Burn it all!"

# BETHLEHEM
## The Little City

The road out of Jerusalem curved around small grassy hills bordered by slender trees. It took a few hours for our caravan to reach a safe distance from the Holy City and I was feeling worse by the hour. We had not been followed but I ached to know what had become of the children in Jerusalem. I knew that my immediate duty was here and as the night passed Bethlehem grew near. In what seemed like an eternity, the new day came and the dawn would be upon us. Just outside of the little town of Bethlehem we looked up to the heavens and gazed upon the King Star. It was a beautiful sight, this quiet town set against the night sky. The King Star was anchored. This was the place for the king of kings—the king of peace.

"So this is Bethlehem," said Majid breaking the silence.

"The city of King David," Balthazar added.

"It's not very big. And it's so still," said Omar.

I turned to my young cousin, "You are accustomed to Jerusalem, a city that never sleeps."

"We will make camp here until we can find the child king." said Majid. "Thank you my son for guiding us."

My father's gratitude gave me some comfort. It had been a stressful journey, and we believed that we had reached our destination. Tomorrow we would search for the new king. I looked up at the night sky. It was expansive and breathtaking. Such beauty; it was clean and pure. It was the greatest of wonders to behold for it was boundless and open to so many possibilities. In returning my thoughts from the heavens and back down to the earth, I reflected on the danger in Jerusalem, the girl, and the odds that I would never see her again. I yearned to return and make sure she escaped and I prayed continually for her safety. I knew that I could never return to that place so long as Severo lived. Nor, could any of us return to this land so long as King Herod should live. I prayed that night that the new king, this King of Bethlehem, might end the suffering of these people and bring new life to this dark and godless land.

We took turns on the watch, more so than usual, and placed our tents, packs and weapons close together. Ra-bi placed the animals a short distance away and over a small sand dune. Despite our hesitation to rest, and the chance that we could have been followed, the ordeals we had been through earlier that night taxed our senses. We were completely exhausted and fell asleep all too quickly.

In the morning, we made our way through the narrow streets of Bethlehem. The people were friendly, many of whom were interested in our journey as if we were important travelers from a large city of even more important people. Little did they know, we were just a group of curious intellectuals hoping to make sense of the stars and trying to determine if it was an omen of greater significance—the promise of the things yet to come.

While I was occupied with returning to Jerusalem, the *Ma-ji* were interested in interviewing several families. My father had made friends with an old man named Zacharias, who became our tour guide of sorts. The old man led us to those, according to the ancient texts, who were listed as belonging to the house of David. One family fascinated us in particular, but the child was much older than we had expected and was only distantly related to the family line. At the end of the day Zacharias invited us to stay with him and his wife Elizabeth, a daughter of Aaron. Later we learned that there were two young boys in the family, one was Zacharias' new son and the other the son of his relation, Joseph. It was Joseph's young boy that the *Ma-ji* found most intriguing.

"Father," I said quietly, pulling Majid away from the others, "I must return to Jerusalem."

"But Zebedeo," he started.

"I promise to return quickly," I soothed.

"I cannot be your savior this time," he added.

"I have been delivered father," I replied, "It is my savior who needs saving."

He gave me a puzzled expression then waved me off and after a moment, turned back to the conversation among the men.

I was determined to leave immediately and rode as fast as Midnight could carry me back to Jerusalem. When I arrived that afternoon, the little house where Rhia and her family lived was gone. Nothing more than a smoldering and charred pile of rubble remained. I dismounted Midnight and stepped over the burning embers. I could see a few traces of the home; the table where I had scorched my mouth with hot tea, the place by the door where I first saw Rhia, and the broken pottery that held the desert roses I had left for her.

I fell to my knees. I had lost her. I wept uncontrollably. It was my fault. All of it. I should have heeded Mary's warning to leave them alone. When I recovered my wits, my eyes reexamined the broken fragments of the pot of desert roses intended for Rhia. There were traces of blood upon them. I could no longer bear the thought of what had happened to her—and to her family. I must face him. Severo and his men must be destroyed.

I traveled to the prison and stood on Midnight's back to peer into the barred window. The last hope was finally extinguished as children were not there. The jail was empty. In the distance I spotted Malcaius talking to some other guards. It was clear that they were preparing to travel and I knew that it was time for me to leave. I wanted Balthazar's counsel. What could be done about this dark creature called Severo? And how did he know that Rhia was gone? What did he fail to tell me?

# RETURN TO
# THE KING
## IN THE CITY OF DAVID

I returned to Bethlehem but the night had fallen. The *Ma-ji* were gathered around our new host and Zacharias was a great admirer of men who traveled. He inquired extensively of their personal histories and wanted to know more about the orient, the *Great Silk Road*, and people in China. To his delight, in the evenings we told stories of our adventures and shared our beliefs and he was not completely surprised that we were familiar with the Hebrew sacred texts. He insisted that we stay in his house, and we were overtaken by the story of Joseph's family, his wife Mary and how they were forced by the census to travel by donkey while the woman was heavy with child. As the story continued, we learned how husband and his childbearing wife were guided by spirits that were not of this world, but prophets of the one and true living God.

It was not long after that we all fell down and worshiped the child known as Jesus. And the *Ma-ji* declared him the future king and deliverer. And in that moment, I understood that this boy was destined to become the great bringer of peace promised by the prophets. While all of us were amazed, I felt the great hope for these people for the final answer to the tyranny that ruled the land was upon us. Each evening we listened to the stories of Zacharias and Joseph, and I came to know my purpose. Yet Balthazar seemed to have an understanding about all of these events even before they were told. This is the king who would conquer the darkness I had witnessed. He would rid us of the Severos and the Herods that poisoned the world. I believed that we were here to protect him; from what however, I had not fully discerned.

Zacharias' house stood on the northern side of the city and only a short distance from the breathtaking hills that bordered the area. It had several spacious rooms with comfortable fireplaces and work areas, a garden courtyard with a great arbor which was ideal for spending time during the hot afternoons, and a rooftop loft that was perfect for stargazing. One particularly warm day, Liu Shang was seated in the outdoor patio behind the house and began teaching the two little boys of the household about the heavens. Gaspar and Miriam sat with the women; Mary, Jesus' mother, and Elizabeth, John's mother.

Majid, Joseph and Zacharias were discussing philosophy and the ancient star prophesies. Earlier, Omar and I had worked alongside the other boys in the family but with so many of us, there wasn't that much to fill the day so we sat in the courtyard too. Balthazar kneeled in prayer a few paces away within the walled garden.

"Master Zacharias," I inquired, "where might Omar and I clean our blades?"

"Please, use the carpenter's bench over there," he replied.

Omar and I set out our gear and I unpacked the small bag containing the star-guide and cylinder, our short blades and scimitars. The two boys, Jesus and John, sat restlessly in Liu Shang's lap, frequently climbing on him and grappling each other while being held in his arms.

"Jesus, John, please don't treat Master Liu Shang that way," Mary called.

"Oh, let them play," replied Liu Shang. "They will be men soon enough."

"How right you are," said Elizabeth. "They have already grown so quickly."

Across the courtyard I could hear Joseph, Zacharias, and Majid discussing the science of building. The poor family, I thought. My father would probably bore them to death and they'd regret taking us in.

"You are men of science and mathematics and I am a man of faith—a humble builder," remarked Joseph. "While my profession does require calculation, I have not your mastery. Your understanding is far beyond mine concerning the stars and their meaning."

Majid interjected. "Let me explain how the stars relate to your profession as a builder Joseph. Stone cutting is a sacred act for it considers our orientation to the equinox, the heavens, and the rising and setting of the sun."

As we sat at the table nearby, Omar picked up the star-guide. Omar might have been naturally good at our craft, but he was a very impatient student.

"Try again Omar," I said. "You can't expect to do it all at once."

"I did it just like you said. I can't do it," Omar cried in defeat. "I will never be a great man of the stars anyway. Why should I try? I'd rather make people laugh. Here, let me tell you another funny story."

"Omar, your stories are not funny."

"What do you mean they're not funny?" he said twisting his face indignantly. "Of course they are. My mother cries laughing every time I have a new tale."

"That is because she is your mother," I teased. "She will always cry when you try to tell stories."

"That's not what I said . . ." Omar's voice wandered off disappointedly.

Balthazar seemed to have finished his prayers and Liu Shang had fallen asleep. The young boys were running around and playfully circling Liu Shang. They quickly darted out of the garden.

"Omar, Zebedeo—would you mind staying with the boys?" Mary asked. "They're curious and tend to wander."

I turned to Omar, "Come." and nudged his shoulder.

I placed the scimitar in its sheath and the instruments in my bag, tossed it over my shoulder and started to follow the boys. I heard Balthazar gasp and looked in his direction abruptly. In his final moments of meditation, Balthazar had seen a vision. I motioned for Omar to go ahead after the boys while I paused at the gate.

"Balthazar, are you unwell?" asked Joseph.

"It was a vision," he muttered. Balthazar stood and turned towards the group.

"I saw a great fire with angry black clouds, smoke and flames as high as the mountains, moving toward my family's house." Balthazar explained. "It consumed everything in its path.

"What is this?" Liu Shang muttered as he awoke.

"And when it stopped," Balthazar continued. "It stood before me and did not waver as if it were waiting like a hunter. Then, with a flash of light like a thunder bolt, a solider emerged from the fire and thrust his sword into my flesh, I tried to cry out and warn the others, but my screams were without sound."

"What manner of vision is that? And very disturbing," said Joseph. "I too had a vision last night. One that I would very much like to forget. I feel that we should leave Bethlehem. But a dream is a dream. It is nothing."

"Sometimes dreams can be God's way of reaching us," said Balthazar. "It is when we are at our softest; our most vulnerable. When a man is awake, he's more likely to reason the message away. Tell me of this dream Joseph."

Balthazar sat down with the group and I could hear no more of their conversation. I turned and followed Omar and the boys who had gone to play and explore as young boys do.

# DISPATCH

## Of Revenge

It wasn't long after I fled Jerusalem that Severo would march toward Bethlehem and preparations to find the child king were well underway. While Malcaius wasn't completely honest with his superior regarding the girl, he managed to convince Severo that resources were thin and Herod's orders should take priority. But Severo was torn. While his men were among the elite, they were few. He had dispatched a small group of men to scour the city for Rhia and her family. But not long after, they were ordered to return. Another small group of scouts were dispatched to search for the *Ma-ji*, and another group he commissioned to search for the child king. Most of the men weren't serious about the pursuit however, and had better things to do like visit their own families and small children. Severo's hold over them was dimming.

"Malcaius," said Severo.

"Sir," he replied stepping forward.

"Send our best scout in the direction of Bethlehem," Severo ordered.

"Your favored scout Claudius was banished by Herod for treason," Malcaius replied. "If anything goes wrong, Herod will know that your alliance with him has been rekindled.

"It is a risk," said Severo. "But very unlikely that Herod will ever discover it."

"So you are certain he should be called to scout for the boy king?"

"Do it." replied Severo. "And stop questioning my authority or I'll have your head."

"As you wish my lord," Malcaius replied.

It was not long before Malcaius went outside the city walls to meet with Claudius. The scout agreed to search for the *Ma-ji* and to give word to Severo directly should he find them. But his price was high and Claudius was uncertain whether Severo would pay him. Circumstances being what they were, things became more and more complicated. Severo sensed in Malcaius a hint of defection but later dismissed the idea knowing that the man was merely ambitious. Severo would need to be steady if he were to deliver the child king and the *Ma-ji* to Herod for punishment. Only then would he have his fortune and his title. Only then would he be satisfied.

Within a few days Claudius had observed the *Ma-ji* in Bethlehem. And apparently they had not seemed to wander around the town much, but were in the company of just one family. Of particular interest to him was the fact that with this group there were two very young boys—boys of the appropriate age of any would-be usurpers of the crown. This was good news he thought as it would mean a quick and nearly silent execution of minor proportions. Claudius returned to find Severo and leave a report of the situation.

But as fate would have it, Severo was in session with the king and could not be reached.

"Claudius, I see you have just arrived," greeted Malcaius.

"Indeed, Malcaius. I seek Captain Severo."

"Alas, I am sorry," Malcaius replied. "He is expected to be in session with the king for some time."

"This is a matter of some urgency, I'm afraid," said Claudius.

"Well then, just tell me your message and I'll make sure the captain receives word."

"Malcaius, you-yourself said that I should deliver any news to Severo himself."

"Gentlemen," said Malcaius to the other men. "Please leave us."

It was generally understood that while Malcaius seemed to busy himself with affairs of state, Claudius preferred anonymity. So the few guards who had been sitting around the room reluctantly assembled themselves and departed.

"I understand the sensitive nature of your call Claudius," Malcaius added. "I have your wages."

Claudius did not immediately take the pouch of gold coins. He looked at Malcaius with distrust. So Malcaius taunted the scout by jingling the bag of coins in front of his face.

"Here you go. You may wish to take them. Otherwise, you may have to wait for days before Severo can pay you, which, as we both know for your sake, might be a little undesirable considering that you are wanted for treason."

They both knew the real reason behind that accusation and Claudius wasn't going to quibble. So with that remark, Claudius snatched the gold and began his report.

"The *Ma-ji* are in the company of the house of Zacharias in Bethlehem. There are two boys of the appropriate age who reside there as well. The family is of the house of David."

"And have these infants concocted a grand scheme to overthrow the crown?" Malcaius mocked.

"I will leave you to your own conclusions Malcaius," Claudius replied. "I have found the child and the circumstances meet Severo's criteria."

"Well splendid," Malcaius scoffed. "I'll tell Severo that you've served your purpose."

Claudius quickly left the room and Malcaius had a few moments to pace alone. But it wasn't long after that Severo entered, weary of his duties in court.

"Malcaius. Any word from the scouts?"

"Indeed, you have just missed your dear friend Claudius."

Severo walked right up to Malcaius' face.

If you weren't my friend I would cut you down for your insolence. Malcaius smiled and Severo struck him across the face.

"He's not my friend," said Severo almost apologetically. "But he has been right in the past."

"It was merely a joke," he replied wiping a small drop of blood from his lip.

"Where is he waiting?" said Severo.

"He will not be waiting. Even for such a man as you, my lord"

"My order was for him to bring any report of the child king directly to me—and no one else! Malcaius how is it that you could not detain him?"

"I can only assume that with a charge of treason on his head, he was unwilling to tarry," Malcaius offered. "But he did leave us with an interesting predicament."

"How so," Severo asked.

"He indicated that the *Ma-ji* were indeed in Bethlehem."

"That doesn't sound like much of a predicament," said Severo.

"Right you are," Malcaius replied. "But the *Ma-ji* wander from house to house and there are many, many boys and they are hidden among different families all of the time."

"You're saying that the *Ma-ji* are hiding the child among different families to prevent us from finding him?"

"I am afraid you must slay the whole lot," Malcaius replied.

"Herod will not be pleased."

"Severo, what does it matter?" Malcaius cooed softly next to him. "Whether you slay one child or a dozen—your reward will be great."

"You are a good soldier Malcaius." said Severo gratefully.

# STAR STONE

## A WINDOW TO THE SKY

Omar was good with younger children and they always loved to hear the absurd stories he concocted. After following the children from Zacharias' house, my cousin and I walked casually behind the boys through the winding streets of Bethlehem. We passed areas familiar to Jesus and John including John's favorite pass, a small walkway between two buildings, which he pointed out for us to follow. The path led us out of the town and to an uphill foot path. We followed the boys to the hillside where caves dotted the landscape. Jesus and John entered a shallow cave before Omar and I could stop them. But quickly we caught up to them, watching them hide in straw-filled mangers. As soon as they were discovered, they jumped out to surprise us. Omar and I smiled. I knew they meant well but I felt responsible for them and had to give them counsel even though they were still very young.

"You boys should not be in these caves alone," I scolded. "A wild beast might eat you, baaah!"

I chased them as they giggled and shrieked. The youngest Jesus, was a very young child but John, was a little older and seemed to understand. They were happy, polite boys and readily left the cave with us.

"An old man lives in that cave," said John. "From Qumran."

"Is he?" I asked. "Well he wouldn't want you to play in his house while he's away. Come now, let's continue."

We walked up another short and steep path and continued near the caves approaching a rocky hillside. The path provided a slim walkway under a collection of dangerously heavy and jagged rocks overhead that looked like they would topple down on us at any moment.

"Omar, take the boy's hand."

I motioned to Omar to hold on to John while I steadied the little boy Jesus.

"This is where a rock fell on a lamb and killed him," John said turning to me.

"Not dead," Jesus said innocently.

"He fell," John replied.

"Enough little brothers." I instructed. "The rocks are very unstable here. Let's continue."

Then, seemingly out of nowhere, an old man appeared and addressed me.

"What the boys say is true," said the old man. "A fiery stone fell from the sky and struck the lamb—like it was a star thrown by the hand of God."

This man's sudden appearance startled us and I felt the need to protect the boys behind me. I placed my hand on the scimitar held at my waist.

"Who are you old man?" I demanded.

But the old fool paid no attention to me and in an instant, walked away.

"I mean no harm to the boys. Nor to you," he announced. "We discuss the word of God and the Holy texts."

He then stopped and turned back in our direction.

"I am a priest like you young man—though you seem intent on making yourself a man of war rather than a man of the heavens."

Before I could say that I was merely protecting the children, the old man turned around again and proceeded forward on the path and turned abruptly to enter a cave. Jesus and John raced out from behind me and followed the old man into the cave. I was alarmed and started feeling that I was losing control of the situation. I turned to Omar, motioning him to come forward. Returning quickly outside the cave in front of us, Jesus appeared.

"Come!" Jesus called.

He motioned with his little hand for us to catch up and then he turned and darted back into the cave.

"Hey, where are you going? I said no more caves!"

But my words fell on deaf ears. I hated caves. They were cold, dark, wet, and usually stinky from a dead animal carcass, filled with bats, snakes and spiders, or worse, someone's unsanitary dwelling. Omar shrugged at me, his faithful expression optimistic. I had no choice but to follow the boys. At the entrance, there rested a delicate brass oil lamp on a shelf made of natural rock. It was a pleasant surprise and reminded me of our home in Tayma. I took the lamp and walked deeper into the cave and with Omar in tow, my eyes gradually adjusted to the difference in light.

We approached a corner and emanating from around the bend we could see a greater light, the light of a large lamp. As we approached, the old man was standing over a large bed of straw, olive leaves, and wild grasses. Standing next to him were Jesus and John. We approached the silent group and witnessed the fallen lamb upon the pile, its eyes closed peacefully. The place smelled of death. The old man and the children appeared to be praying silently.

"Omar, gather some wood and we will prepare the burial fire," I whispered.

I didn't want the boys to overhear and lament our decision. Children could get so attached to animals, treating them as royal pets and I didn't want the disease of this dead animal making us sick.

"Wait my friends," said the old man softly. "Where is your faith?"

"He is finished," I replied.

"There are stones that kill, and there are stones that bring life. Was it not through a rock that Moses gave the people water?" said the old man.

"Life-giving stones?" I huffed. "Omar, the wood."

I felt a tug at my garment and there standing next to me was little Jesus. Omar and I looked at each other puzzled as we did not see the boy move from the old man's side. I looked down again at the child. He extended arm and I held out my own in response. He beheld a stone that measured the entire width of his tiny chubby hand—large, round, flat and polished, clear like water with the brilliance of a gem from the royal court.

"I am a rock," the child uttered.

"You *have* a rock," I corrected.

The child's statement was cute but he was still a babe learning the language.

"You found the star stone!" John delighted.

"For you," Jesus said smiling up at me.

"It is beautiful," I said accepting the stone. "Thank you. Peace to you little brothers."

At that instant the lamb stirred from his bed and rose from the pile of vegetation. The boys laughed as the lamb hobbled toward the cave's exit. Omar and I stood astounded; mortified.

The old man extended his arm in friendship. "I am *Ya-ir*," he said.

"Zebedeo," I offered clasping his arm and still in shock.

Omar followed the children closely outside the caves and I followed with the old man. We stood looking out on the pastoral view below while I tried to reconcile the oddities that I had just witnessed. I watched as Omar and the boys were competing to see who could toss the farthest pebble out to the valley.

"God has given us everything we need to live a good life," Ya-ir said to me breaking our silence. "But, the law is only as good as man is to uphold it. And many times we fall so short. I fear that someday, all the secrets and true wisdom will be lost."

"What kind of secrets?" I asked.

"The lamb you saw, struck by a rock and left for dead?" Ya-ir tested like a schoolmaster. "Yet now, after three days he lives. Has God provided a miracle? Or has he given us a message?"

"Would not some in your tribe call that blasphemy?" I questioned.

"You are right," he acknowledged. "But perhaps something like love should replace the law."

I looked at him puzzled. I didn't understand where this was leading.

"You have the stone?" he asked.

"Yes."

"It is the same tool as the one given by the Almighty to Enoch, used to foretell of the great flood," Ya-ir said. "You are the young Zoroastrian—the *Ma-ji* of the stars?"

"My father." I corrected.

"And you have your tools. They help you read the heavens?"

I nodded and noticed that the old man said '*read the heavens*' when most men ask if I observe or study them. This was a particularly interesting matter because my father and many Zoroastrians claimed to have the ability not only to study but to *interpret* the meaning of the stars, eclipses, formations, the equinox and their signs and omens. They make careful calculations and predictions based on ancient methods and observations. Ya-ir knew more about the heavens than I had given him credit. He was starting to scare me. Maybe he really was crazy.

"As you use these tools," he continued. "There is an ancient verse you may wish to know.

*Two holy stars in heaven when the morning star is born.*

*This triune will guide you to the path of righteousness and life everlasting.*"

"You speak with hidden meanings old man," I said frustrated by his philosophical puzzles. "I do not understand your legends!"

"You have your tools, God has His. Take yours to God," he said starting off in another direction towards the caves. "With the light of the rising sun you will discover God's message."

I tried to ignore the way that Ya-ir made me feel—haunted. So rather than become angry, I merely dismissed him as a crazy old man, collected the boys, and made our way back to the village.

The sun began to set and while we walked, I thought about the day's events. Some people might be intrigued by the wonder and miraculous recovery of a dead animal, but I found it a little eerie that it was supposedly dead for three days. As I replayed what had happened, I realized that the old man may have been the guardian of some ancient secrets, but I had neither patience nor a desire to understand.

# THE LAMB

## IS WITH US

The room was quieting-down. The little boys were already hard and fast asleep. The fire in Zacharias' great room began to dwindle with its low hisses and crackling sounds. In the adjoining chamber, I could hear the elders preparing to sleep. Omar and I were bunked next to each other not far from the great room fire.

"Want to hear one of my funny stories now?" said Omar. "You'll really like this one."

"No. I told you. You're not funny. Maybe you could be a great a butcher or a blacksmith someday but not a story-teller. Go to sleep."

"Just one—really quickly?" He pleaded.

I did not answer which possibly gave him liberty to begin anyway.

"A man was visiting his friend's farm. When he arrived, he noticed a lamb with a leg made of wood . . ."

"You said this would be quick." I scolded.

"It is. It is. I promise," he said innocently.

I made a yawn as if not paying attention and closed my eyes. Omar continued.

"He was very curious of this lamb and asked his friend, *'How did the lamb get a wooden leg?' 'Well, that is a very special lamb my friend,'* the farmer answered. *'He chased away a wild boar that attacked me.' 'So, the wild boar tore up his leg?' 'No,'* replied the farmer. *'Ok, so how did he get a wooden leg?'* His friend asked. *'Well,'* the farmer said, *'you cannot eat a special lamb like that all at one time!'*"

He waiting for me to laugh but I pretended to sleep. Omar paused hoping to gauge my reaction to the tale. But I didn't want to encourage him to pursue storytelling—it wouldn't profit his life and truly was an art reserved for the old men. I believed that I was forcing him to grow up, and while he resisted, he would benefit. Resigned at my silence, he turned over and went to sleep. I peeked at Omar with one eye, his eyes were closed. I smiled at his innocent expression and rolled over to sleep.

# POINT OF ORIGIN
## BEGINNING OF THE FUTURE

It was early morning and still dark in Bethlehem when I had the first vivid dream. I recall seeing a blur and movement in the darkness, and then I heard a muffled and distant scream, fire and smoke. I realized that I wasn't breathing and woke with a panic sitting up in my bed.

Omar stirred but did not wake. I looked at my cousin with affection—twelve years old and so much to learn about life and responsibility I thought. I rose and picked up the star stone and the star-guide—fitting the stone in an open notch on the device. It didn't quite fit. I lifted the scope made of brass and attached the stone to the end of it. I climbed the small wooden ladder to the rear roof pointing away from the town. It was calm and serene. The night sky was gently fading and the cusp of the dawn approached. Like our home in Tayma, the roof top was a special place for me and a place where I could engage my thoughts, my prayers, and relish my wildest hopes. I prayed that the children I had left were safe. I felt they must have survived the fire and wondered if they escaped Severo's prison as I had.

I looked to the heavens and recalled the words of the old man.

*'Two holy stars in heaven when the morning star is born;*
*This triune will guide you to the path of righteousness and*
*life everlasting.*

*For in the light of the rising sun you will discover God's*
*message.'*

I pointed the scope to the heavens and released a joyous sigh because to my astonishment I viewed the universe with greater clarity. Two large planets appeared in retrograde. The diagonal they created, aligned with us, was no coincidence. I knew exactly at that moment what the old man was trying to tell me, this was more than a miracle, it was a message—a metaphor. The morning star is the Deliverer . . . so what does the rest mean? I had to wake Balthazar.

An unusual smell of wood burning caught my breath. In the same instant, a male villager burst into the house below me shouting.

"Take your children now! Flee while you can!"

I ran to the ladder and dropped down without use of the steps, holding to the sides, and obtaining many wooden thorns in my hands as I descended. The villager ran away but the door remained open. I could hear the women screaming and saw them running past the doorway. Houses and out buildings were on fire, men were trying to put them out and families with infants and small children were running in a chaotic frenzy.

"The children? Why would they harm the children?" Joseph exclaimed in disbelief.

Balthazar joined me and quickly approached the doorway. I followed behind him as we stepped outside the house. Balthazar grabbed the arm of a villager running by.

"What is it?" Balthazar demanded.

"Herod has ordered the slaughter of all male children," the man cried. "Come now or your little ones will die!" We stepped back into the house and closed the door.

"Herod's assassins," announced Balthazar.

"Assassins?!" said Majid.

"They will show no mercy." Balthazar confirmed.

The elder's faces said it all—frozen in their disbelief, fear and confusion.

"They have come to destroy the child king," proclaimed Majid.

Instantly, we awoke from the fog that had petrified us and gathered our things. I placed the stone in my garment near my breast and thrust the star-guide and scope into my bag. Omar was awake—barely, and still sleepy and confused.

"Cousin, you must move quickly," I commanded. "You will come with me."

"Zebedeo, take the children to the caves," said Zacharias. "Find the old man he will know where to hide. Hurry, and do not look back."

The women started mourning and weeping, upset to be separated from the boys.

"Mary," Joseph consoled. "They will be faster through the city without the women." And turning to the children he said, "Jesus, John, do as they say. Hide and we will come for you soon."

And they kissed and held the boys lovingly. As my father and I witnessed this display of family affection, we could not help but be moved. He turned to me with outstretched forearm.

"Trust in heaven," he said.

"I will," I replied, grasping his arm.

I took Omar and the two small boys out the front door and turned to head towards the caves.

"Gaspar, take the women through the back," said Balthazar. "We will meet you at the hilltop."

"I will stay and fight," argued Gaspar.

"Not now my cousin," comforted Majid. "We need someone to help the women. And war does not suit you."

Gaspar conceded the truth and agreed reluctantly.

"Trust in heaven," Majid added.

"I will," said Gaspar. "Do not delay or we will fear for your safety."

Gaspar led Miriam, Mary and Elizabeth out the back door. It was a longer route, but it was easier for the ladies to climb the slow-rising hills.

# INNOCENT

## A Bloody Path

As we stepped out of the house, we realized the severity of the chaos. Herod's elite guards had become brutal assassins sent from Jerusalem. They besieged the little town of Bethlehem singling out infants and small children. And while targeting males, they seemed to kill just as many girls—either to make a point, or to be as thorough as possible.

The women were fighting off the attackers as much as the men. They would not give up their babies so easily. Like vicious cats cornered, these loving parents would die before letting any villain take these innocents from their arms. But the force and brutality of these men of death overpowered them. While the assassins pulled a child's leg, the mother would cling to the rest and as soon as enough of the babe was free, the assassin's would stab, and cut, and destroy. Rivers of blood seeped down the roadways. The villagers' pitchforks, hoes, and sticks were no match for metal armor, heavy swords, and metal tipped razor sharp spears.

I took Jesus and Omar held John and we raced through the crowded streets. We were fighting against the masses, a frenzy, and moving against a current of horrified villagers hoping to escape the slaughter. Within moments, a small group of assassins saw us with the boys—the primary targets of this raid.

"Hey, you there, stop where you are!" an assassin ordered. And like the obedient innocents they were, the boys froze in their steps.

"What are you doing? Run!" I declared to the boys.

We moved forward against the hundreds of villagers running in our direction. With the massive flow of panicked mothers and fathers, the running mob served to block our attackers for a time. Looking back, I could see the *Ma-ji* in front of the house. Balthazar had his scimitar drawn and stood slashing Herod's assassins one by one with razor sharp accuracy that spurted blood in high arcs across the footpath. He finally made his way towards a woman screaming to protect her baby. An assassin was about to kill the woman and child with his dagger when Balthazar hacked the assassin across the neck. The villain cried out in agony then fell to the ground in a bloody heap.

Majid and Liu Shang tried to intervene but they could not save the neighboring children. Two lean assassins chased a couple of small boys who ran away in terror. But the assassins pierced the children in the back as they fled. Horrified by the coldness of these men's hearts, Majid followed the men from behind and struck one assassin with several lethal blows of his scimitar. The assassin tried to retaliate—but it was too late and he fell to the ground. The other assassin was on fire thanks to the quick thinking of Liu Shang who had ignited some black powder and blew it into the assassin's face.

The villagers continued to pour into the streets and now many of the old, weak and small were being trampled by the mobs. I turned to pull Omar and the boys into a small alcove waiting for a break in the frenzy and watched as Majid had moved on to another set of assassins. Zacharias and Joseph emulating Liu Shang improvised by taking torches and tried to battle the assassins with fire. An unsuspecting assassin, moving in to slash a child with his sword, was torched by Joseph. His cape and tunic caught fire and he howled away in flames. At the same time, Zacharias was waving off an assassin with his torch but encountered the sharp end of the assassin's spear, piercing his side. Joseph quickly grabbed Zacharias and led him away.

In seeing the attack on Zacharias, Liu Shang followed boldly after the assassin. He methodically pulled from his vest a set of razor edged Chinese darts. Liu Shang threw them forcefully into the elite guard's body, one of which pierced him so fully that he was pinned to a wall. The man was close to his end and pled for the sage to end it. The Chinese elder honored the villain's request by piercing him through the heart with his own dagger.

Balthazar was in his element. He had acquired an assassin's heavy shield and after using its edge to crush an attacker's face, he swung it around by a strap to cover his back with such swiftness that it looked as if it weighed no more than a dried leaf. He was assaulted by several assassins now, busy fighting all of them at once—a spear in one hand, his scimitar drawn in the other, and the shield covering his back. He moved like a cat and loomed above them up the stone steps like a god.

From across the square I saw Severo standing next to Malcaius watching the mêlée. Doubtless he had ordered this attack on Balthazar. Malcaius soon left the Captain's side. Within moments, Severo's eyes met mine and he ordered several men to seize us. Balthazar watched as they moved toward us and became wildly furious. Just as he started after Severo, two more assassins lunged forward to attack him. It was enough time to allow Severo to escape.

I took the boys and ran down the narrow streets ahead of Omar who followed closely. As the assassins gained, I pushed Omar ahead and moved to hold-up the rear, enduring several blows to my head, face, and arms. The pace continued and seemed an eternity. Assassins were on my heels, hacking and chopping everything and everyone in their path and the streams of blood spattered my face. In my attempt to hold them off, my scimitar was knocked from my hand. My bag was gone too, along with my scope and star-guide. We took side streets and alleyways but could not dodge them. Fortunately, our attackers were laden with heavy armor and we scaled obstacles that they were too slow to navigate. But as they violently pursued us—our hearts were racing and we felt our end was at hand.

"There!" John called out remembering his familiar path.

He led our group down a narrow alley toward the caves. Through the windows, I saw the horror of helpless screaming women whose babies had been ripped from their hands. We passed others who had been cornered. In their madness, a few villagers had frantically clawed the stone walls in an attempt to escape the horror until their fingers were nothing more than bloodied stumps.

"The passage—," little John called out.

John's usual short-cut through a narrow passage was blocked by rocks and we had to turn around and instead take a narrow foothill with a steep incline, barely scalable. The path led us to a small chasm passable only by the long wooden beam that bridged the gap. Above us stood a crest of jagged rocks and below lay a steep cliff to the other side.

We passed over the beam only to find a dead-end near the rocky cliffs and we realized we'd need to turn around again. It wasn't detrimental I thought, we had outrun them. But as I turned, I saw that somehow the assassins had followed us. We were cornered—trapped. The boys shook in terror as the assassins closed in, but I was proud of them. They had been so brave. They had worked together to escape. They had inspired me.

And in that instant I was more determined. The enemy would have to go through me first. I pushed the boys further behind me. I would confront this enemy, giving my life just like the parents I had witnessed. The assassins paused, waiting for their orders as Severo approached. As I stood waiting for their move, Omar darted out from behind me and ran towards the closing assassins.

"Omar!" I shouted.

Omar ran to the heavy beam that bridged the gap. I understood his intentions, but he didn't need to do this. He stooped to lift the board and dragged its cumbersome load awkwardly way, cutting off the enemy's path. They could not cross the chasm. Omar gleefully started back to toward us near the crag. Severo, angered by the set back commanded his men.

"Kill them!" he declared.

At that moment, I saw their faces. They were hesitant, reluctant, and exhausted. They realized perhaps in that instant that they were soaked, not in the blood of a foreign enemy, but of thousands of innocents. These men had their own families and their own children. They were weary and now questioned their leader and their mission. This slaughter was unjust and evil. Hesitating, they looked at each other. Severo, in disgust, instantly pulled a spear from a guard's hand and hurled it in the air. And in an instant it was over. Omar was pierced through his back and out through his heart.

"No!" I cried uncontrollably.

The sound of my pain was so loud that the echo resonated through the hills and caves around us. The men trembled and a bit of gravel fell from the cliffs above. I grabbed Omar just as he fell, holding him in my arms. I could see his expression, his innocent eyes, and his surprise that the good deed he had felt joyous over just moments before, was cut short by a sinister one. I tried to stop the bleeding, but it was too late. Omar's fate was certain. I fell to the ground and held Omar in his last moments.

"Zeb?" Omar croaked. "Have we saved the boys?"

"You have saved them Omar," I comforted. "And tonight you will tell me all of your funny stories—for I am eager to hear them."

"You never liked my stories Zeb."

"You are wrong my cousin, I have loved every one."

"Even the wooden leg?" he asked.

"Especially the wooden leg," I said.

"I'm tired," he said with a sigh and closed his eyes. His last breath exhausted.

Through my sorrow, I whispered, "This first born son joins his father in heaven tonight. I will miss you cousin."

# BEHOLD A STAR
## WHO WILL LEAD US

My despair turned to rage. As I rose, I saw Severo ordering his men to find something to place across the gap. Several assassins brought a narrow and frail piece of wood. They started to place it over the gap and attempt to cross the chasm. I looked around to find something to knock the boulders above loose. There was only small gravel and sand underfoot. Then I remembered the stone in my garment. I pulled it from my breast and held the stone high for the enemy to see.

"Wait! Do not cross," I shouted.

The soldiers froze at the other end of the slender beam.

"For if you do, the hand of God will strike you down. I swear it!"

I held up the star stone and all the men wondered. I too wondered—did they take my actions as a ruse, a trick, or sheer foolishness? But I caught the eye of Severo who now seemed more interested in the object my hand beheld. It was clear now that this must have been the object he asked for in the prison cell. I could see it in his face.

"What are you waiting for?!" Severo commanded. "Get that man! I'll feed his corpse to the crows!"

As they rushed toward me my heart raced, the seconds seemed to stall and my thoughts turned towards my cousin, my father, the girl that I loved, and the two small boys shuddering behind me in terror. The elders say that when confronted with death we will fear no evil because God is with us—it is peaceful. My life had passed before my eyes and in this moment, I faced a certain death. I wanted to pray as Balthazar had taught. For an instant it crossed my mind. But I felt enraged, not at all peaceful. I acknowledged my blessings to God and snapped out of the foggy mess. My thoughts were perfectly clear. I lifted my arm back and threw the stone into the towering rocks above us with every ounce of strength that I had. The rocks wobbled for a moment and then they unsettled completely and made their way downward like a great wave in an ocean storm.

Their wickedness had been answered. Skulls were shattered, bodies splattered, and the assassins fell to their death below. Moments later as the rubble and debris cleared, I was relieved to see that Balthazar was running up behind the place where the assassins stood; his scimitar drawn and bloodied. He had beaten them. But our relief dimmed quickly. Between us now stood Severo; dusty but unscathed. The wave of tumbling rocks had missed him entirely. The Captain looked at Balthazar, much in the way an ambitious man looks upon an honorable challenge that could define his own greatness. But honorable men are defined by a certain set of rules, none of which Severo strictly adhered. Yes, Severo was proud, but he knew precisely how to defeat this man.

"Let's finish this," Balthazar growled.

# MADNESS

## OF MEN'S HEARTS

Severo struggled to be his own man. He knew the risks of
disobeying Herod and perhaps extended things a bit too far
now and then, testing Herod's tolerance of his unorthodox
ways. And while Herod had authorized Severo's actions, the
attack in Bethlehem was escalating. Herod feared Rome
would notice and intervene. That morning Malcaius,
attempting to save his own skin, had fled back to Jerusalem
to advise the King.

"What is it?" Herod demanded. The second in
command had traveled directly from the battle scene, his
attire torn and his body bloodied.

"In Bethlehem sire, the men are deserting," he said.
"They feel the attack was unjust. There was an unholy
tension that pervaded the air, your majesty. The bloodshed;
screams of women and babies—it's a horror."

"They are assassins," he said rising to his feet. "Severo's elite. Now they cower because the farmers waive sticks at them? My orders must be obeyed!"

"Severo has not followed your orders sire," said Malcaius. "He and the criminal Claudius had planned to slaughter all of the children rather than merely capture the child king as you ordered."

"Traitors!" shouted Herod in a fury.

"Killing innocents, the wickedness of it, has stained their souls and driven the troops to madness," replied Malcaius. "The men have left the city and roam the wilderness like beasts."

"Where is Severo?!" Herod demanded. "I shall have his head. Clean up this mess before we have the entire Roman garrison on our doorstep. Promise me you will not fail."

"I will not fail you sire," assured Malcaius.

Malcaius was pleased with himself. Severo would be blamed for the chaos. He took his leave and backed out of the throne room as Herod continued to shout.

"I am Herod the Great. There shall be no other King of the Jews!"

The great man fell to his seat and clutched his heart in pain.

Back in Bethlehem the sun reached the midday sky and in the wilderness the assassins fled the town crying in shame and self hatred. Bloodied, they threw down their swords, helmets and spears and began to tear at their clothes and hair. But the ends justified the means in Herod's eyes and it all could be explained—Severo had gone rogue. He would take the blame. Thousands of children were dead and hundreds of others along with them in their defense. It was a dark day and a dark moment. The child king and future deliverer was in the midst of the battle and was about to be slain at the hands of the enemy.

Zacharias' wounds would need attention and he had lost a lot of blood. The women were weeping as the children had not arrived at the caves. Gaspar was doing his best to calm the women by starting a fire, and bringing them inside. As the day progressed however, everyone, even Ya-ir whose faith had always been completely steadfast, began to pray fervently.

# LET'S FINISH THIS

## MAN TO MAN

Mourning overcame me and my failure to defeat Severo and protect the children was suffocating me. Omar's death was certainly my fault too. I returned to my cousin and shielded the boys. As if in a fog, I watched as Balthazar slowly approached Severo. The battle would be painful, Balthazar was strong but Severo was wretched and sinister and would trick Balthazar in order to win. There would be blades and scimitars, spears and shields hurled at one another. They approached each other and there was no doubt in my mind that this was an all or nothing match, where only one man if any, would walk away alive.

Severo was fully armored and began with a quick swipe of his sword followed by an immediate jab with a spare helmet he held in his hand. Balthazar was ready and defended against the sword, but the helmet grazed his face as he dodged. Again and again the men lunged forward, savagely attempting to cut each other with a blade or spear, dodging backwards from the blows, and defending themselves with the battlements left behind by the fallen assassins. Through careful footwork and masterful tactics, the men appeared evenly matched. It was the most difficult thing for me to watch—both were strong, handsome, and full of promise. Both were agile, fearless, and able. But I knew their hearts. One was composed of pure good; and the other the embodiment of pure evil. My knowledge was my fear. And my fear included knowing that sometimes evil wins.

Balthazar, a masterful student, studied Severo the way a predator studies the movements and habits of its prey long before striking. He smirked. I knew that meant he had found a weakness. At the right moment, Balthazar distracted his opponent with the shield then followed through with his spear at an angle and struck Severo in the head ripping his helmet off. As it flew, Severo's brow was cut and the open wound gushed with blood. His pride and vanity were exposed—otherwise he was barely wounded, and he seethed with hate. He fell to the ground on one knee grasping the sand to steady him. Balthazar lunged forward. On rising, Severo threw sand in Balthazar's face then struck him with his shield. Balthazar was thrown off balance, and his body was hurled toward the cliff. The earth crumbled beneath him and Balthazar, about to plummet to his death, gripped the ledge with his bare hands and tried to find his footing on the jagged cliff face. Severo approached the ledge and towered over his victim. Balthazar could not get stable footing and every time he found a rock or crevice to support him, the sandy soil would give way.

"Zebedeo!" shouted Balthazar.

Severo loomed over him.

I leaped up and grabbed the wood beam that Omar had dragged from the gap and lifted it to one shoulder and swinging it toward the captain as fast as I could, certain that my eyes were closed out of panic and clumsiness—but it worked. The beam broadsided Severo across the face and sent him stumbling away from the ledge. It looked as if he had been knocked out as he lay on his back in the dust and rubble. From the corner of my eye, I could see that Balthazar was lifting himself up and was no longer in need of my help.

But by then, Severo was recovering and started to rise. I quickly replaced the beam, breached the gap, and picked up a spear as I crossed. I leaped upon the villain before he could rise further and stood over him with the spear to his chest and my foot on his neck.

"Wait!" he croaked. "Did I not show mercy when you were my captive?"

I paused. Hesitated. My father taught me that everyone has the capacity for good or evil and a single act can create a life or destroy it. What distinguishes us from those who seek evil rests in our ability to act righteously in the face of death. I thought, isn't mercy and forgiveness the mark of true power and righteousness? Was I better than this murdering fiend who would kill innocent babies, tearing them from their mother's arms? Yes, I was. But I was no fool. This man was not only a liar, he would never repent. Severo began to pull a dagger from a small sheath on his leg. But my foot remained upon the villain's neck and I pressed it down upon him further.

"Did you show mercy to the rug maker and his wife?"

He grew visibly angry as I shocked him with my words.

"Did you show mercy to my cousin with your spear? And did you show mercy to the mothers and children slain in this hour? You must answer for your crimes you filthy goat!"

Severo moved to mortally stab me in the thigh. But I was ready. I lifted the razor sharp spear and pierced his chest—straight through the heart and straight through the goat crest. Severo cried out. Blood curdled down his cheeks and out of his mouth as he choked on his own blood. The mouth of the goat crest mirrored its master and the blood pooled in the sand beside him. Our enemy was dead.

# TRUST IN HEAVEN
## And You Shall Live

I rejoined my family and friends at the caves outside the town that afternoon. Mary helped care for Majid and Liu Shang's injuries while Elizabeth tried to soothe Miriam's agony over the loss of Omar. Joseph helped old Zacharias get comfortable but it was clear that his wounds were beyond our help—his life was in the hands of God. Ya-ir kept watch next to the hay-filled mangers where Jesus and John safely slept. I watched from a distance as my father was speaking with Ya-ir privately. They seemed to be in each other's confidence and my father bowed deeply to the old man and I thought I heard them say,

"We are in this journey together, forever, always. Amen."

But maybe I was just imagining it. I was too far to really hear and frankly, I probably should just mind my own matters. My father left Ya-ir and returned to helping the wounded.

Outside, Gaspar, Balthazar and I helped the other men lay the shrouded white forms of hundreds of little children along with those adults who perished trying to save them into a wide mass grave. The last body Balthazar and I placed in the grave was Omar's. Gaspar cried. Many women were at the site crying. I leaned over Omar and with the black liquid I had saved, I drew upon the shroud directly above Omar's heart—a picture of the King Star and the symbol of the *Ma-ji*. Liu Shang approached and laid a sealed clay jar beside Omar.

"A relic of the *Ma-ji*," said Liu Shang.

"Trust in heaven," I said. "Rest in peace."

"I am sorry for the loss of your cousin," said Balthazar.

"His sacrifice saved the new king," I replied.

"If Herod lives to his name, there will be more sacrifices made."

"I dreamed of this night and knew these events before they happened," I said.

Tears were welling up in my eyes despite my fight to suppress them. But Balthazar understood.

"This loss is felt by many men tonight," he comforted.

"How can I be a man with such tears?"

"A true man has the courage of a lion and the kindness of a lamb, and the wisdom to embrace each at the right hour."

"The child must go to Egypt," I said collecting my emotions. "It was clear in my dream and it is the only way the boy will be safe so long as Herod is alive."

"It will be done," Balthazar replied.

I slept very little that night and preferred to keep the watch, under the stars, while the others slept peacefully in the caves. In the morning, my father stared at me when I entered the cave and seemed different; unquestioning, as if in silent approval.

"We make ready for Tayma my son," he said while struggling to lift his heavy pack.

"Let me help you with that," I replied.

"Thank you warrior-priest," Majid said to me with a grin.

My father's embrace was welcome and the firmness of his arms fulfilling.

"You are a man of the *Ma-ji*, protector of the new king" he beamed. "And you have shown me that the old ways are not the only ways."

"Thank you father," I replied. "The Deliverer is safe for now but I think we should watch over him in the times to come."

"Indeed," said Majid, "but for now we must send him on his way."

Joseph, Mary, and the boy were prepared for their journey to Egypt. Gaspar and Miriam agreed to stay with Zacharias and Elizabeth. It would be a few days before Zacharias could travel, but they would join the new king in Egypt soon. Everyone had been willing to take our counsel after the bloodshed and we were anxious to leave Bethlehem.

"I am sorry for the loss of your star stone," I said to the boy. "I wanted to keep it to remember our friendship."

"Remember," Jesus said pointing up to the sky cheerfully.

"Yes I will. Peace to you little brother." I lifted the boy to his mother on the camel and turned to join my father who was counseling Joseph.

"If you must live in exile as Zebedeo has advised, Egypt is a good place." said Majid.

"Take this gold," Gaspar added. "Your family can trade it in the marketplace and no one will ask your business."

"Thank you," said Joseph.

Liu Shang approached and offered his gifts. "Silk and incense, oils and herbs, these small gifts will adorn your family and heal your wounds."

"I have no gifts worthy of a king only those of a humble priest," Balthazar said apologetically to Joseph. "Here is frankincense and myrrh from my homeland along with my pledge to honor you each day in my prayers."

"Your gifts are great blessings to us and our hearts are overjoyed," said Joseph. "Zebedeo, my words cannot express our gratitude. You are an angel of God. In the face of death, you showed great courage. Blessings to all of you on your journey home."

Balthazar mounted Eclipse. Liu Shang mounted his camel and my father turned to me with a sigh.

"I am sorry to have been so hard on you my son. You have proven yourself worthy of the Order."

"You are a good father," I replied. "What is the Order?"

Majid grinned without answering as I helped him take his seat upon his camel.

"I think we'll follow a new road—just to be safe," said Liu Shang.

"Indeed. And I shall lead the way," Balthazar added.

"I don't think so my friend," replied Majid. "You're likely to get us lost."

I smiled and shook my head.

"Last time you led were nearly killed by thieves!" claimed Balthazar. "I shall lead us."

Liu Shang added, "I will lead us east and then . . ."

But he was interrupted.

"Zebedeo will lead you!" Gaspar shouted from a short distance. "He has earned the right above all of you silly women!"

And as we laughed together Gaspar and the others waved us on. We headed toward home looking to the heavens and the star-lit sky. After a time, I looked back and saw the faint image of Joseph and his family heading toward Egypt.

"Go in peace little king," I said softly.

# RETURN TO TAYMA
## THE ROAD AHEAD

Our caravan traveled several weeks through the northern hills and then south through the deserts of foreign tribes until we neared our homeland. I welcomed the sweet comforts of home and the simple life we had led. And despite my ambition of remaining the same after this journey, the truth was, I was altered. And as we neared our land, the men became active and playful. I heard Balthazar joking with my father. Liu Shang's understanding of their silliness became second nature and he started harassing Majid and Balthazar in equal measure.

We arrived at the residence before nightfall and were greeted by Joshua, Rhia, her cousin Mary and the little children. To my pleasure, they had accepted my invitation to stay with us. My little note was not lost afterall. And in their gratitude, the children had cleaned and whitewashed the house, cleared the stockyards, repaired the barns and planted the gardens. Joshua and his brothers and sisters stood at the gate looking so well that I had barely recognized them. Rhia was stunning, perfumed and seemed very happy. As I approached, I could see that she wore around her neck the slim leather cord and small wooden star that I had placed on the note.

The men in our caravan dismounted and my father and the others greeted them with gladness and a commotion of conversations ensued. Joshua explained my invitation to his family and showed Majid all that he and his little siblings had done to improve the property. The men and women walked around the side of the house to the farmyard and left me behind with Rhia. I could barely contain myself for my smile was so wide that I surely looked like a fool. Nevertheless, I calmed myself and tried to approach her patiently.

"From the first moment I saw you, my heart was no longer my own," I gushed with excitement. Apparently, I forgot to compose myself entirely.

"Even when I was a dusty little maid?" Rhia teased.

"Especially when you were a dusty little maid," I replied. "Do you recall the question I asked of you in the letter?"

"I have thought about it every day," she said softly.

"I beg your answer woman," I said with a laugh.

"Yes. A thousand times yes."

In an instant I swept her up and whirled her around in my arms. I was the happiest of men. And so this ended our adventure surrounding the arrival of the new king. But this was not my only adventure to tell but one of many which, in time, I will recall with all the details and particulars of interest. You see, the times since then have changed—our circumstances altered. The men of our time no longer understand us. They seek not to understand the mysteries of the heavens nor the powers of God. And my fear is that the generation to come will be strange to us and will push us aside as bewildered old men. The years will pass and our secrets will be lost, just as my father and Ya-ir had predicted.

In telling my story I hope to honor Omar. I hope also that men in the time to come will understand our journey and our conflict. In that moment, we were not wise. We were not kings. We were men.

And in my old age I write these words as my good wife and I sit on the rooftop each night. We look to the stars and share our adventures with our children and our children's children and their children too so long as God will allow. My one regret is that I never returned to Bethlehem to retrieve the star stone that gave me a glimpse of heaven and saved us that day. Perhaps its power was best left buried in the past. And I believe that whoever discovers this message; to him the mysteries of life shall be revealed. For, we are in this journey together, forever, always. Amen.

# ACKNOWLEDGEMENTS

This story is a work of fiction inspired by the word of God, the Holy Spirit and my Lord and Savior Jesus Christ. The history was inspired by the writings attributed to St. Matthew at the time of Christ's early life, the ancient Roman records and census, and the life of King Herod the Great. The portraits of the characters that appear in this work however, are fictional, as are many of the events described.

Many friends read versions of this book in manuscript form, and I am grateful to all for their insights and encouragement. In particular, special thanks to Darla Catalfamo, Daniel Angers, Jeremy Regal, Bill Alfonsin, William Kamstra, Judith McCormack, Lulu Fairman, and Saundra Nicholson.

I would like to express my sincere appreciation to the pastors at Calvary Chapel of Costa Mesa for their sound teaching of the Gospel, their love, and faithful guidance and in particular thanks to Pastor Chuck Smith and Pastor Greg Laurie (now at Harvest Fellowship) for without them this work may not have been possible.

And finally, I would also like to thank my family, the thousands of fans of *Crescent Moon* on Scribd, and the Publisher's editorial and creative teams for their support in this endeavor and their belief in my ability as a writer.

Here's a sneak peek at

# ORDER OF THE MAJI

The thrilling sequel to *MAJI*

# TRIBUS FAMULUS
## Welcome to the family

Rhia and Mary were behaving like little children—giggling and talking, secretly they huddled together and shared whispers as they planned the details of our wedding ceremony and feast. It had been a month since we returned from Bethlehem and it seemed as if my father and Balthazar were making plans of their own—showing no concern over the upcoming influx of a large party of friends and family who were traveling to Tayma for the occasion.

It was difficult to stay away from Rhia each day as I wanted to spend every waking moment with her, and that evening I would sleep like a child myself. While my routines would soon change with a wife, what a strange thought-a wife, my routine was much the same as before our travels. Each day I would work with the other men of the stars and each evening we would pray, dine and retire for the night.

One such night, I had fallen into a deep and enduring sleep. Well before the dawn, I heard the vague sound of footsteps and voices in my room. The noise must have been very loud as it woke me from a place far beyond normal. I came up from my sleep in the way a dead man would have rose from the grave. Before I could clear my eyes, two dark figures held me down while another threw a dark cloth over my head. I gasped for air. Their arms were strong and I tried to free myself but the force of these villains was too great and began to cry out for my father and Balthazar. Seconds later, the scent of mint and pepper was upon my face and I immediately lost all sense and direction.

Some time later, it may have been days or hours, I did not know, but I awoke to the feeling of sluggishness in my head. I wondered if I were going to die here. After all that I had been through, this would be a sad twist of fate. Judging by the awful bitter taste in my mouth, I was confident that I had been drugged. The cloth was no longer covering my head and I was seated in a chair and unbound. As my eyes adjusted, I beheld what appeared to be a cold and empty stone room—dark and foreboding with the musty smell of decay engulfing it. I needed to find a way out before my attackers returned.

"Stay seated," said a voice in the darkness.

"Father?" I answered. "Is that you?"

A single spark from a stone and blade ignited a candle. It was placed on a long wooden table and cast a sinister glow along the faces of the men. Seated behind the table like a panel of judges were Majid, Balthazar and Ya-ir, the old man I met at the caves near Bethlehem. They wore white robes with a symbol similar to the one I had drawn on the chest of Omar and like the one I had drawn on my cheek with my uncle's black ink. I wasn't as original as I had thought. I had seen this symbol as a child.

"Zebedeo of Tayma," said Ya-ir presiding. "It is your time."

"Time for what?" I replied. "Father what is this nonsense?'

"Zebedeo," Majid announced. "We are the Counsel of the Order."

"The Order?" I repeated, still groggy from the spirits that drugged me. "What's the Order?"

"The Order of the Ma-ji," Balthazar continued. "You must first go through the purification ceremony and follow with the Trials of the Twelve."

"I don't understand."

"If you live through the Trials of the Twelve," Ya-ir added, "then you will take your place of honor in the Order."

Balthazar placed a dagger on the table. Majid placed a book on the table and opened it. Ya-ir stepped forward with the candle and lit a small mound in front of me. The fire took to the fuel quickly and its light illuminated the room. I could now see a hole in the high ceiling allowing us a glimpse of the stars above. Ya-ir had returned to his seat at the counsel table.

"Zebedeo," Ya-ir commanded. "Do you wish to take your place among the Ma-ji?"

"Of course I do," I answered. "But I thought I already proved that back in . . ."

"You have shown some interest, my son," replied Majid. "The proof however will come with fire and water and blood."

"Wait, blood?"